THE LOBSTERMAN'S
DAUGHTER

Also by Michael Lieberman

POETRY
Praising with My Body
A History of the Sweetness of the World
Sojourn at Elmhurst
Remnant
Far-From-Equilibrium Conditions
Bonfire of the Verities

FICTION
Never Surrender—Never Retreat, A Novel
of Medical Politics in Texas
The Women of Harvard Square, A Novel
in Short Stories (Fall, 2014)

THE LOBSTERMAN'S DAUGHTER

Michael Lieberman

Michael Lieberman
Summer, 2014

Texas Review Press
Huntsville, Texas

FIRST EDITION, 2014
Requests for permission to reproduce material from this work should
be sent to:

> Permissions
> Texas Review Press
> English Department
> Sam Houston State University
> Huntsville, TX 77341-2146

I thank Ruth Irvin for copy editing and managing the production
of this book.

I thank Brian Kenneth Swain for his close reading of the
manuscript and thoughtful comments.

Cover and drawings by Nancy Parsons, Graphic Design Group

The Lobsterman's Daughter is a work of fiction. All characters,
events, and places are products of the author's imagination or
are used fictionally. No resemblance to actual people or events
is intended.

Learn more about Michael Lieberman and his work at his
website: www.michaellieberman.com
Contact him: poet@lieberman.net
Facebook: www.facebook.com/michaelliebermanpoetwriter
Tumblr: www.michaelwlieberman.tumblr.com

Library of Congress Cataloging-in-Publication Data

Lieberman, Michael, 1941- author.
  The lobsterman's daughter / Michael Lieberman. --
First edition.
      pages cm
  ISBN 978-1-937875-59-6 (pbk. : alk. paper)
  1. Families--Maine--Fiction. 2. Maine--Fiction. 3. Family
secrets--Maine--Fiction. I. Title.
  PS3562.I434L63 2014
  813'.54--dc23

                              2013039630

For Seth Shulman

Contents

THE LOBSTERMAN'S
DAUGHTER

Foreword

When Henrietta Markham walked into my office half way through her junior year at Harvard to plan her honors thesis, I had no idea what a remarkable young woman she was or, even by the standards of today's young people, what a lurid imagination she had. I remember thinking after our first meeting that Eris had marked her as surely as she had set in motion the siege of Troy.

What is reproduced here is a revised manuscript—perhaps "testament" is a better word—she sent me the spring after she graduated. It bore a Barcelona postmark but no return address. The document is an edited and extended version of her thesis; it is even edgier than the original. The new chapters at the end appear to move her work from fiction to memoir or even confession, though with Henrietta one can never be sure.

There is little I can tell you about her. In class she was a lively contributor who was precise in her phrasing but not acerbic. At times she was a bit abrasive but not beyond what I am used to seeing with my more determined undergraduate writing students. More importantly she was open to exploring her voice without embarrassment or precondition. She had not developed the chitinous exoskeleton I so often encounter in MFA students. In our one-on-one conferences she was warm and communicative though she shared few personal details. I once asked about her family, and she said something to the effect of, "Professor Breathwaite, it will all be in my manuscript." Then she added, "When I'm finished, you will understand. You will read it." It felt more like a command than an observation. It goes without comment that at times she could rankle, purposely I thought.

The packet came with a brief note that thanked me for my help and asked that I try to get the manuscript published, "As a record of my disgrace and my family's." She added that at her first opportunity she planned to go on a silent retreat to explore the possibility of becoming a novice with an unspecified order of nuns. Of course I was stunned. We had read Simone Weil in class, and I imagine that like many impressionable young women she was overtaken by the fervor of Weil's commitment and the power of her prose. I am certain she meant the manuscript to be her final word on this period of her life.

The new version jettisoned the old title, *Expiation,* which now seemed too polite, too academic. But the one she chose was too revealing of the story's end, so I have called her book *The Lobsterman's Daughter.*

I made numerous efforts to track her down—all without success. My emails to three different addresses bounced, and attempts to call her cell phone failed. All I could wheedle out of our registrar's office was that there was a Henrietta Markham from the Boston area who had graduated "within the last five years." This was news because the story is set in Maine and purports to be based on her own family. The bounced emails, discontinued cell phone, and lack of a return address made it clear that she did not want to be found. At this point I put aside the manuscript.

Over the summer her piece nagged at me. I would be at the Harvard Coop, and as I read the dust jackets of the new fiction, I would think of her work and imagine a book of hers displayed there among the others. Or I would be at my computer working on my own fiction, and something she had written would intrude on my story. And so I enlisted the help of my agent and began to look for a publisher. Fortunately she found a small press in Texas that was willing to undertake this project.

What you have just read is the original foreword for *The Lobsterman's Daughter*, however, when I got my set of page proofs back from Texas, I realized that Henrietta had added an epilogue I somehow had not seen before. Other than saying that this coda also holds surprises and is the deft work of a remarkable talent, I will let her words speak for themselves.

Olympia Breathwaite, Ph.D.
Cambridge, Massachusetts

Prologue

This book is a work of fiction though it is based on actual events in my family going back as far as my great, great-grandparents, Dov-Ber and Sadie Markstein. The general outlines of the narrative are faithful to the stories and remembrances of my parents and grandparents—though I have animated the tales of the older generations and that of my father by imagining dialogue and certain details. Of course the story is told in my own voice while attempting to portray what my ancestors thought and felt about their times—and ours, a liberty I freely took. Perhaps this gambit will seem foolish, but for me to tell this story, it feels deeply necessary. With respect to my own life and the lives of my still-living family— my mother Penelope Standarian Markham, my grandmother Riva Botstein Markham, and my uncle George Markham—their words and stories are paraphrases of notes I took while we talked or I wrote down from memory immediately after we finished. The story of my twin brothers Evan and Hank is reconstructed from a long conversation with them, my memories of them, and conversations with my mother. Where possible, I have corroborated and augmented older information by consulting newspaper morgues—principally those in South-Central

Maine—and archived tapes of radio broadcasts where available. My own story, of course, is in my own words though I have allowed myself certain omissions and circumspection of detail. The title speaks to my journey. For it, I thank Professor Olympia Breathwaite, who has been a tireless mentor and an unstinting advocate.

I begin with a partial reproduction of my family tree to help you follow the generations.

Henrietta Markham
Barcelona, Spain

Houston, Texas

The Markham Family

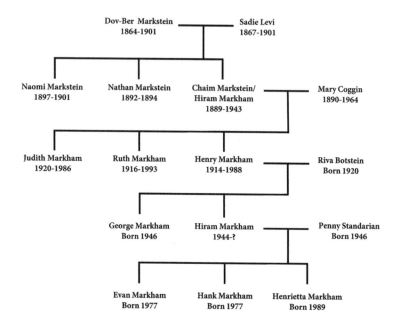

Dov-Ber Markstein
1864-1901 —— Sadie Levi
1867-1901

Naomi Markstein
1897-1901

Nathan Markstein
1892-1894

Chaim Markstein/
Hiram Markham
1889-1943 —— Mary Coggin
1890-1964

Judith Markham
1920-1986

Ruth Markham
1916-1993

Henry Markham
1914-1988 —— Riva Botstein
Born 1920

George Markham
Born 1946

Hiram Markham
1944-? —— Penny Standarian
Born 1946

Evan Markham
Born 1977

Hank Markham
Born 1977

Henrietta Markham
Born 1989

I

Hiram Markham

I don't know when exactly I came to consciousness. It must have been gradual, the seeping in of awareness that with time congealed to clarity. At first the only certainty was the blackness. Slowly I realized I was on my back, wedged into a box with a wicked strut digging into my spine that made movement unthinkable. It didn't matter. I couldn't turn left or right. There was a slight flex to my legs, which forced my knees against the top of the container. I pushed forward hard with the toes of my sneakers, but they met an unyielding solidity. I ran my fingers along the side—wood, wooden slats. Some sort of crate. It was becoming clearer. The distinctive blend of smells—diesel, sawdust and crustacean—confirmed what I have known for some years: my sons are what my grandfather, the first Hiram Markham, would have called *mumsers*, bastards, rotten bastards. They crated me in our work shed. Caged me. Strange what comparisons roil the puzzling mind. I thought of the chain-linked madness of Hephaestus and the score he settled. Poor lame bastard. How justified was his net. Aphrodite and Ares were getting it on, cuckolding him, and he settled a score. Enough said. But me—I have done nothing to those twins, nothing but nurture them.

They must have slipped something into my beer at dinner and carried me out here. I was in one of the big traps that we had built specially for the new lobster boat some years back. Oversized with oversized struts to withstand the heavy seas. With the fall in prices we hadn't used them recently. These pots were stacked in the back of the shed. Or at any rate all of them had been until, I guessed, last night. They had stuffed me in like an oversized lobster and left me. I could feel where one of the slats was splintered and wearing. One of the newer traps, I imagined. What else could it be? They were the only ones big enough. It was still pitch black. But of course it would be in the shed. Its few windows were grimed over and obscured by gear. Morning would come late here. What were they thinking? I have never even raised my voice. Dinner had seemed okay. No one said much—not my sons, not the one wife who was there. We sat and ate in silence and half-listened to the jabber of the T.V. I remember the beginning of a movie. A high-speed chase, the cops trading shots with some guys in a pickup. And that's it. And now, at whatever time it is, I am their prisoner.

No, no way they could have put me into one of the traps. They have no lid, only the netted hole in the side for the lobsters to climb through. Can't be. They must have built one special, put me in, and nailed it shut. Used old wood. Thrifty bastards. Premeditating sons of bitches. Why would they do that? They planned it. Right under my nose they planned it. Built it. No, they could have pried the slats off the top last night and put me in. Am I a pagan in my own house, no better than Queequeg, encoffined by my idiot sons? Worse, Queequeg's coffin was measured and cut, mine a slap-dash, ill-fitting affair. Stupid bastards.

No telling what they were thinking. Then I shouted, "What are you thinking? What are you doing? Let me out." Sparkles barked a little and stopped. That was all. Maybe they couldn't hear. The shed door was closed. From the house they couldn't hear a thing. I shouted louder, "Let me out of here, you bastards." Nothing.

The beer made me want to pee. Badly. I was wedged in tight, no room for anything. I tried to turn. The pain where the strut ground against my spine was a pitiless rejoinder. I could not get my hands to my fly. Just wait. When they come, you'll get out and pee. Ever tried to think of other things when you have to pee badly? I tried doing numbers in my head—working my way through the times tables. I got to 26 x 26, and then on a lark I said to myself, How about 27 x 29. Okay 783. Well, let's just check, 28 x 28 is, what? 784. Fine, the world wasn't crazy. It's those bastards. Numbers still worked. But I did have to pee. The doctor told me my prostate is enlarged. That explains, he said, why I have to pee so much. That and the beer. It was not diabetes. And by the way, not prostate cancer either. What about Pi? Yes, 3.1415926535. Oh, let's just round it up to 654. That wasn't helping much. It was still dark. Saturnine dark my old classics professor might have said. I'll say just "dark." So no one's coming soon. That's what it was, all right, saturnine dark. And my bladder ached. I couldn't hold it much longer.

When I was on the boat, I used to pee off the side if we weren't moving. That worked. And now, even if I could get to my pecker, I'd have to do an Old Faithful, just let her rip straight up and suffer the consequences. Well, at my age it won't be quite old faithful. Yes, yes, the capital of Estonia is Tallinn. I could use a Tall Inn just now. I'd walk in and motion impatiently. No, that might scare the pert young thing at the desk. I'd start by explaining that I'd like a room and that my luggage was in the car, but first could I use the men's room? Thank God I thought of Tallinn. It really solved the problem. Oh, no, here it comes, like it or not. The Old Faithful version gone whimper and right into my work pants.

I must have drifted off. Then I heard voices outside. I opened my eyes, and I could see a little daylight through the filthy windows. I shouted at them again to let me out. What did they think they were doing? "You bastards, let me out of here at once." I heard them undo the latch to the shed. The door opened admitting a gloomy shaft of light. I heard the scuffing of boots on the wooden floor. "I don't know what the hell you think you're doing, but I expect you to pry this thing open. The joke's gone far enough." I heard something scrape against the trap near my head. Later I figured it must have been a belt buckle. There was a slight shaking and then a sense of lift. The contraption swayed as they carried it outside and a bump when they set me on the ground. The yard was not as flat as I thought. All those years I'd assumed that the staging area between the shed and the dock was flat. But no, it was actually canted. And I was slightly head-down. That and the salt breeze coming off the water told me my head was bayward, my feet pointing, or rather crabbed toward the shed with the road behind it.

I figured I had a chance anyway. They would leave, go out to tend the traps or into town. I could shout when I heard cars coming on the road. Someone would come by with their windows open or in a convertible. I would shout, and they would stop and spring me. I hoped the stench of urine would not drive them away. Not likely, just your own prissiness. They would see the injustice, warm to the task, and begin to set things right. At first they would be stymied. I'd tell them to get the crowbar hanging on the far wall of the shed. Even a woman could pry the trap apart with that. No, they would have to start with the rope the twins used to cinch it shut after the nails. No problem, there were shears right beside the drill press. I'd be out in no time, and they could drive me into town, right to the police station. Well, there was the stench. If they were squeamish about their car seat, I could take my mackinaw off its wooden peg and sit on it.

It was very quiet for a long time. Finally I shouted, "I'm hungry." Nothing. I hollered that I wanted breakfast. Nothing. Then I heard the kitchen screen door bang and footsteps. "I'm starved," I said. They dropped something down onto my chest and left. I couldn't tell what it was at first because I couldn't get a hand up. I shook and squirmed, and finally I felt it roll off my chest. I struggled to work a hand close enough to grasp it. I was just able to get two fingers on it. Tenuously I lifted it, not sure what I would do since I couldn't get it to my mouth. My best guess was an uncooked hot dog. Then it slipped and fell. When I reached down again, I couldn't find it. Must have fallen through the slats. Shit. I was wedged into this oversized lobster trap, my muscles cramped, my pants soiled, and I was having a food fantasy.

What I really wanted was a piece of blueberry pie, not made from those fat, tasteless painted whores grown in the South or imported from Chile, the ones that say *Produit du Chili* on the package. I made a mental note to look up the trade convention that specified that produce should be labeled in English and French, even when it comes from Chile for God's sake. All the years I lived with Penny, my wife Penelope, I pretended not to like blueberries. That made no sense at all. None of it made sense beginning with why they laced my beer last night. Then I thought, *It could not have been the beer.* I opened the bottle myself and drank from it. What I wondered, the coffee? Maybe. Blueberries. I wanted a piece of pie made from those small sweet berries that get picked here in the summer. With a good flaky crust. Like the one that Wilma served me that night and claimed she made herself. Maybe she did. I had my doubts, but as things turned out, it didn't matter. Oh, it was good. Wilma, Wilma, I miss you.

I heard them start the diesel on the boat. They let it warm for a few minutes. There was a discussion about an extra thermos of coffee and some new mesh traps they had bought. There was a clunk as they put the boat in gear. The engine ran at little more than an idle. They must have been backing out slowly. It was louder and faster, and after a while it trailed off. Not a car on the road. Too early, I guessed. I waited and passed the time naming the capitals of African countries—Praia, N'Djamena, Luanda, Gaborone, and, let's just say for fun, Cairo. At the end I threw in Palermo. Not quite a capital and not quite Africa but close enough. I made a note to visit when I finished with those bastards. I heard someone coming. It sounded more like a car than a truck. Not a diesel for sure. "Help, help me," I screamed as loud as I could. Nothing, I just heard the pitch lower slightly as the engine faded.

I repeated this with each new vehicle maybe three or four times, no goddamn luck. On the last try I heard the kitchen screen door bang again and the shed door open. How could this be? They were supposed to be on the boat. Somebody was rooting around for something. Then they left. Who? Maybe one stayed behind or the wife. I listened. There was a swish, swish as they worked the kerosene pump. I heard the splat of liquid hitting the bottom of a can. Then footsteps, and suddenly I felt the cold greasy liquid run all over me. "You bastards, this has gone far enough. Stop this at once. If you do, I'll not press charges when this is over. We'll just forget it." The screen door banged shut.

Look on the bright side, I said to myself. The kerosene will mask the urine when I'm rescued. Another car came by, and I shouted my lungs out. "For God's sake, help me. Please." The car faded. I judged from the sound that it was headed south toward Fosterport. It didn't matter anyway. The screen door slammed again. Then I heard the radio. They had put on the radio by the shed door to drown me out. Bastards. Some local station. At least they could have put on

NPR or the classical music station. I get twang, twang, and ignorant opinion. After a while there was the weather. A high of 68 and a virtual 100% chance of rain. Moderate ocean swells of 6 to 8 feet. Local news: Tourism was good this week with area merchants reporting sales up 6% over last year. PFC Dwight Damian Forester had been killed in Iraq by a sniper. Arrangements were pending. And people should be on the lookout for Hiram Markham whose family has reported him missing. He wandered away from the family compound Friday afternoon. He is 67, with white hair and brown eyes, 5'7" and 150 lbs. He has Alzheimer's and can be contentious. So that's what they were telling people. Stupid bastards. Let me just remind you of the house of Tudor ending with Elizabeth I, then the Stuarts, James I, Charles I. Charles II, James II, and don't forget the interregnum. Alzheimer's my dendrites. "You Cretan bastards."

Radio or not, they are not going to shut me up. Not a chance. When I heard what I thought was a small truck coming I shouted louder than ever. I'd show the bastards. Nothing. For a moment there was a bit of a break, some signal failure at the station, and a tractor was coming. I hoped it had no cab. I let out a "Help me" like never before. I heard the tractor go into neutral. I tried to shout again, but now the radio was blaring bluegrass. Jesus, I hate Earl Scruggs. Over it, I heard the tractor go back into gear and move on. Shit. This time when the screen door opened, there were footsteps, a pause, and then the staggered gait of someone lugging something. A grunt, a swish and an instant later the smell of gasoline as it cascaded over me. The lugging moved away. "Bastards, sons of bitches. I'll get even, I promise." The steps came back. I felt the sharp poke of a finger jammed into my ribs. "Bastards." The steps retreated and the screen door banged.

I could hear a boat far out and then closer. Finally they docked, and I listened to noisy camaraderie. The screen door slammed against its frame, and after a minute I could hear what I thought were muffled voices conferring. They turned the radio off. They came by the trap and shoved something through the slats right in front of my face. There was no mistaking what it was. A butane lighter with its long barrel at my nose. "You bastards, get me out of here at once. You, sons of bitches, now. I mean it. This has gone on long enough. At once, do you hear me? I'll shout until someone comes. You can't stop me."

"If you don't shut up, we're going to cook you red as one of those frigging lobsters."

They moved away. I could hear them unloading the day's catch. It began to drizzle. They went into the shed. I heard them getting out of their boots and slickers. The shed door closed, and the screen door creaked. It rained harder and harder, and the temperature dropped. My teeth started to chatter. The cold made me pee. The rain came in right through the slats and pelted my forehead and cheeks. What didn't come though at first collected on top, rolled off, and landed in great plops in my eyes. It was moving toward dusk. And the rain did not let up. I imagined them preparing dinner. I imagined chicken and mashed potatoes, peas, and pie, blueberry pie. Which brought back Wilma again and that evening long ago. I wish it hadn't ended as it did. She made great pie. She was a good person. I wish I had shown more restraint.

They couldn't know this. They were not even born. It was put up as a runaway, and from time to time she was remembered fondly in church or by her parents. Later I married Penny. We had the kids and raised them—the bastards who nailed and cinched me in here. And our daughter, Henrietta.

Sometime in the middle of the night after it had stopped raining, I heard the screen door bang again, footsteps, and then the shed door open. The night was still except for them putting on their rubber boots and slickers. They came back outside, picked up the trap, and carried me down to the boat. They struggled to get me on board, but of course they managed. Then the engine started. They let it idle, and after it was warm, they slowly backed away from the dock.

II

Photograph

There is an undated photograph of Hiram Markham—the first Hiram Markham—and Mary Coggin Markham, a posed shot probably taken at a studio in Lewiston, a formal shot preserved in a family album. It seems to be a copy, which would explain why there is no date and place noted on the back. Many of the others in the album bear the neat script of a woman's hand, most likely Mary's. If she had annotated the photograph, we might imagine: "Hiram and Mary Markham, Lewiston, Maine, June, 1913." That would have been the year before their son Henry, my grandfather, was born. If Mary is pregnant, it is hard to discern in the photo. She was twenty-three and he twenty-four. Nineteen-thirteen is many years before their grandson, the other Hiram Markham, whose unfortunate end you just witnessed, was born.

We should observe this photograph with some care, for it may contain clues to what strain of madness ran and still runs in this family.

He is trim and erect in a black suit and stiffens his right shoulder slightly to accommodate her hand, which sits upon it, exposing her fingers.

These take a triangular shape and reach just over his suit coat. He stares straight ahead out from under a bowler which looks slightly too small and perhaps is a photographer's prop or borrowed from a friend. He looks dapper in a buttoned black vest and bow tie. Is that the gold chain of a pocket watch attached to the third button of his vest? Perhaps it indicates that our Hiram is a stickler for detail or punctual, or do we simply see a man caught up in the fashions of the day?

The light slants from his left and leaves the right side of his face, the side on which Mary stands, in shadow. Should we assume this to mean that part of his life is opaque to Mary or that he has something to hide or that the photographer has a set routine and Hiram and Mary were yet one more customer that busy Saturday afternoon? He has a small *boutonnière*. Perhaps they are celebrating their anniversary, or is it a nice touch, part of the services of the studio to add a level of finish to the portrait? His hair is thick and black under the bowler, and he sports a pencil thin mustache. Altogether the effect is somewhere between Charlie Chaplin and Errol Flynn. At this point in our story, we wonder if the neutral look on his face as he stares straight ahead is the cover of a master, that, like Chaplin and Flynn, he can play a part well, or simply the chance shot the photographer selected.

This is no hint of dis-ease in his bearing unless it is that he grasps the edge of a table to steady himself. While this pose could be the work of the photographer, we have to remember that Lewiston in the first part of the last century was a small place, and it would not do to have everyone in town arranged the same way. Yet so far as we know, there is no reason that he should have to assure his equilibrium. He does not beat his wife, nor is he a drunk. He has no gambling debts and has committed no crime. So we may take this attitude as well as the way his shoes are splayed at a right angle to reveal a slight unsteadiness in his role—a way to secure his position in an uncertain and hostile world. We cannot say whether it has anything to do with a certain anxiety about the circumstances of his upbringing or the state of his business. It is unlikely that the affairs of the world— the atrocities of King Leopold II of Belgium in the Congo, the bitter and bloody struggle of Victoriano Huerta to seize control of Mexico, the churnings in Georgia that will shortly lead to the resurrection of the KKK, the unrest in Europe that will result in the assassination of Archduke Ferdinand of Austria and the collapse of the continent into a senseless war, and (this is most important for our story) temperance stirrings at home that will bring prohibition—are troubling his brow this afternoon. But there can be no doubt: Hiram Markham is working at composure.

And Mary? Mary's face is pretty, yet clouded with anxiety. She is tightly cinched at the waist in a black dress with a lacy fringe at the bodice where the black fabric overlays a white blouse. On her face too the light courses from her left, but her face is much more revealed—as if she has less to hide or is less good at concealing conflict or perhaps just less troubled. She wears a gigantic hat, a fantastic hat, vaguely like a Turk's turban, of fur or fabric. It is as if a permanent black cloud moves with her. Only a bit of her dark hair shows beneath. We know of nothing in her past of which she should be ashamed. What is unknown is the future. But she has no reason to fear it, and even if she did, it would be too much to believe that a photograph, especially one taken on a Saturday afternoon in a photographer's studio in Lewiston, Maine, could reveal the future. Altogether she is an attractive woman with nice features—a determined mouth and large arresting eyes—and a good figure. The lobe of her right ear emerges from the shadow, an unexpected detail that defines the right side of her head from the darkness. Her right arm is slightly askew of her side, and her hand grasps the material of her dress seemingly to pull it back a bit to reveal her figure. As we noted, her left hand rests comfortably and confidently on Hiram's right shoulder. Close inspection reveals an elaborate wedding ring.

A first impression of the backdrop is that it shows a hint of a large building with a steeple that seems to rise out of the top of Mary's hat in line with her right eye and a second, fainter, in line with her left. The overall impression is of a structure hinted at as in a Turner landscape. We must not overinterpret this motif since the photograph is faded and we may be looking only at trees and shadows in the mist. Moreover, we have no way of knowing why the photographer chose this backdrop for the handsome young couple. We must also wonder if he knew the couple, their habits, their proclivities, their family backgrounds. Remember, Lewiston in 1913 was a manageable small town, and only a certain class of people would have used his services. We cannot know what to conclude. Even if there is such a building, the faint air of Christendom or poshness or European elegance lent to the scene by the backdrop may be completely accidental. Perhaps this is his only backdrop—other than stark white—or only the best fit among a very few. We cannot say if he is trying to capture anything and if there may be some dark significance to the composition that with our present knowledge we cannot grasp.

An odd and unexplained feature of the photograph is the sense of triangles the photographer has captured—first the fingers of her left hand on his shoulder, then the shape of her right hand as it gathers her dress. Her wasp waist and her right arm and his right arm define two others. His suit and the crook of his left arm constitute a fifth. It is only now that we realize the photographer has also backlit the scene. These triangles may simply be an artistic touch, something he has learned at a course in Boston or by trial and error. Whether we should attribute any significance to them is unclear, any more than to the flowering branches of a tree to the right or the decorative motif of the base of the table which Hiram uses to steady himself, though the flowers do add a sense of innocence and simplicity to this couple, which at the same time is withdrawn by the elaborate figuration of the table base.

We noted that both Hiram and Mary are dressed in black, but they are not in mourning. The effect may be an artifact of a rescued old black and white photograph or part of the formality of the era, that getting dressed for a formal photograph a hundred years ago carried much more weight that it does today, when even the point and shoot has been replaced by cell phone cameras. Mary seems engaged, determined, cautious perhaps, but not sad. Hiram is stiff and even secretive. He looks as if he is about to whistle through his lips in relief at not being found out. But we do not know what he worries over. Perhaps he does not know himself, or that even now he knows he will cloud his future with certain actions that he cannot anticipate but that he is sure will occur. We may marvel at the power of photography to reveal what is hidden from the participants in this drama—but we should not make too much of it. When we say it is the power of art to unmask, surely we do not mean to unmask evil that has not yet occurred. If there is anything improper about these two, it has certainly not occurred when this posed photograph was taken.

Finally, consider what looks to be a half-face or mask just to the left of Hiram's left elbow and half encircled by the curving trunk of the ascending, blossoming tree. We cannot be sure, but it is as if there is a third person, or part of a third person, or half of a Greek tragic mask in the room, although calling attention to the face in this way might give too much weight to our little drama. Yet it is there, a harbinger of something although we cannot be sure what. The line of the photo's crop bisects the nose and face sharply as if to suggest that we are getting only half the story. The face does not ask for patience on our part—that is something we must supply ourselves.

We have now seen the grandparents, Chaim/Hiram and Mary, and we have heard from Hiram, their grandson—and we know about his daughter, Henrietta, the last of his children.

It is clear that this family story must unfold by degrees. We are ready to meet Chaim Markstein/ Hiram Markham and then his wife Mary, who are captured in this photograph.

III

Chaim Markstein

My name was Chaim Markstein. I know you are wondering what I am doing here. Well, I thought I would give you a little history so you would know a little more about my grandson Hiram and his disappearance. To begin with I had better tell you something about me. You will not find anything anywhere about "Chaim Markstein," which was the handle my parents affixed to me at birth, but I am getting ahead of myself. There is nothing to tell you about them, Dov-Ber and Sadie Markstein, except that I wish to state decisively and without regret that my father was not a rabbi or a scholar. When you listen to the stories of Jews in the Pale of Settlement—including Poland where the Marksteins hail from—it is hard to imagine how any cows got milked or wood got chopped. Everyone was learned or on his way to being so. I say "his way" because of course the women did not count. No, my father was a horse trader. I had some vague sense of that when I left, but I must have put the story together later. At six you do not really know much about your parents. Still it was hard to miss the horse shed—I cannot dignify it with the word "barn"—behind the house or the auctions. I imagine, like the rest of us, he had a head for numbers. Else how would he have survived in that cutthroat, *goyishe* world?

Well, not to take up too much of your time and to come to the point, for reasons that were always unclear to me, my parents sent me over alone as a child to a distant aunt and uncle, Aunt Betty and Uncle Bernard Lovett. I do not remember what port I left from, or what train we took to get there. There were just the three of us. My younger brother Nathan had died of whooping cough the year before. Back then, it was not clear to me whether it was fear of pogroms or superstition about my brother's death or simply the desire for a better life that set events in motion. They promised to come the next year, but I was to go ahead and learn, as they put it in Polish, "to be a Yanqui."

The year was eighteen and ninety-five. This is a lot of detail, but be patient. As they did in those days, my father pinned my name and the Lovett's with their address in Lewiston, Maine to my jacket. They took me aboard. I cried then and later as the ship pulled away. I never saw them again. Somehow, they never came—that year or the next. Letters arrived in Polish that the Lovetts could not read. At first they found no one who could decipher this old-country text, or at least that is what Aunt Betty told me. As I look back on it, she knew much more than she let on. She must have found a *landsman* to translate their letters. I would get only vague reports that my parents loved me and all was well. The only real news was that a few years after I left they had a daughter, Naomi.

That is all I knew until much later when I learned the final, terrible truth—and it was only reluctantly that Aunt Betty told me. I was sixteen. A few years after I left, my father had accused a Polish horse trader of swindling him, and when he would not make it right, in a fit of rage my father strangled him. Strangled him. I do not have to tell you the rest. It was Poland in the early twentieth century, and vendetta was the law. Actually I do not know the details of the horrible aftermath, only that Aunt Betty said the Poles made an example of him and my mother and Naomi. They barricaded them inside our house and burned it down.

For a few months I felt deeply sad. But bit-by-bit their memories faded. It took a long time to realize how utterly alone in the world I was. At six one remembers so little to begin with. And by the time I knew they had perished, I was older and used to being on my own with the Lovetts. Yet I had a deep, nagging sadness. Why had they never come for me? There was a second worry, an even deeper one that inexplicably gnawed at my insides. Could I ever do something like that—lose control and strangle someone in a volcanic rage? No, I did not think so. Like all kids I got into some fights in the schoolyard, and some were worthy of a bare-knuckle prizefight. It is also true that in fifth grade, I stomped on Billy Walker's face and sent him to the hospital, but that was only because he called me a dirty kike. I guess there are also other things I am not proud of, but they are not necessary for you to know.

To return to the story, the Lovetts were there at Ellis Island when we docked. I spoke only Polish at the time and a little Yiddish. Fortunately Aunt Betty knew a few words of Polish and some Yiddish from her mother, and that got us by. They drove me to Lewiston where they lived. On the way my aunt said I could not live in Lewiston with a name like Chaim Markstein. Since my parents were to come next year, this was all a little delicate. She said, "We are going to call you 'Hiram Markham.'" The Lovetts must have discussed it beforehand, but I cannot imagine my parents knew. I think Aunt Betty assumed that they would become "Dov-Ber and Sadie Markham" or maybe "Dennis and Sally Markham." And that is how I went to school and then to the University of Maine. Another thing, I never legally changed my name. Things were different then. You simply did something. There were few rules and fewer people enforcing them. I never regretted being Hiram Markham. Of course, people knew I was Jewish, but it was a bit easier to get by in school and in college not being Chaim Markstein.

Turns out I had a talent for math. Numbers came easily to me, and so I became an accountant. Perhaps I set my sights too low, but at the time— remember I went to college in nineteen and seven—it never occurred to me to be an engineer or an economist. Of course being an accountant then was difficult too. Nobody hired Jews in those days. What saved me was Mary Coggin. Her family had a hardware store across the river, the Androscoggin River, in Auburn. I guess you have noticed that I am a detail person—which was good since I was an accountant. Imagine if I had not tended to rows or columns—somebody would have been in a pickle. Mary Coggin's family. I worked for her father and took the business over when he died. There I go again, getting ahead of my story.

The Coggins lived on our side of the river, and I took a shine to Mary in high school. She was a year younger, and good-looking. Really though, the Lovetts and the Coggins arranged it. They made a match, though everyone was so busy trying not to be Jewish while being Jewish that no one said they made a *shidduch*. There were not too many eligible young Jewish men in South-Central Maine then, and, well, I was presentable. I came over young enough to speak without an accent, and I had gone to college. I say that they arranged it, but it was fine with Mary and me. We liked each other, but looking back, I cannot say I courted her as people did later. We fell in together, a couple a kids, green to the world, and eventually we married.

All of this seems a long way from my grandson, the other Hiram Markham. "Hiram" was more popular as a name when the Lovetts gave it to me, and "Markham" was a name that sounded good to Aunt Betty, I suppose. The whole thing, "Hiram Markham" with no middle name was a contrivance, but not different from someone in their family changing Liebeskind to Lovett.

The family got to lobstering in the damndest way. I brought my fiscal knowhow and a natural mechanical bent to the Coggin's hardware store. We did pretty well, and eventually we had a little money. Mary and I hankered for a place on the coast for the summers. Of course, in the winter it did not matter. It was cold and gray and always snowing. But the summers were marvels, a time to frolic away the slough of winter, if, that is, you were on the coast so as to avoid black flies and mosquitoes—but only if the wind was right.

Well, the summer place. It was near Fosterport on a quiet bay. I must say I am plenty proud of myself because it did not look like much when we bought it from a local family that had lobstered from it back many years. It was more of a camp than a gentrified retreat. The center of the place was a large shed, a staging area in front, and a dock on the other side. An old lobster boat got thrown in as well. The house was nothing to speak of, a two story, charmless structure covered with brick shingles. And there was the rest—a privy, a kerosene barrel and pump, a rusting tractor—I never could figure why they had it. They had no land. There was also a dilapidated stable a ways back. Somehow, it never got torn down. Well, bit-by-bit we modernized the place— put in a cesspool and flush toilets, dug a new well, replaced the shingles with white clapboard, and repaired the stable behind the shed. We kept the boat and lobster pots. And a little later I bought a new one, or rather I bought a used one from the wife of a neighbor lobsterman who had died.

Mary would spend the summer with the kids, and I would come down weekends and when I could get away. My son Henry and I learned the basics of lobstering from a neighbor. I never really did much. I would take the family boating, but it was mostly getting out on the bay, not actual lobstering. Then the most unexpected thing happened. Henry, let me see, he must have been about nine when we bought the place, Henry got interested. His younger sisters teased him, but they were glad to dip the succulent meat in melted butter. They fancied city life. Not to get diverted, but they ended up marrying and living in Boston.

So lobstering was accidental, how it got into our family. What I thought of as a summer retreat, Henry came to regard as a lobster camp. And of course, at a place like Bowdoin, which is where he eventually went to college, his head got stuffed full of Thoreau and Emerson. As for *kashrut*, kosher, it never came up. My family could not spell it.

Mary and I had a good life. Prohibition hardly bothered us. We did not drink much to begin with, but I procured some Canadian whiskey and that did us for the occasional Saturday night drink and party. Then the KKK got active in Maine though they seemed focused on the Catholics and those with French-Canadian names. Now the depression was a different matter. I always said to Mary that I was glad we bought the place on the coast when we did, because when things got bad, although they never got really bad, when things got bad, I never would have spent the money. We cut back some at the store. I made ends meet as I could. I had to be inventive, take some risks, offer more credit than I wanted, barter some, but we did all right. You know, being foreign born, deep down, I feared there was going to be a pogrom, but it never came. No, we were doing fine raising the three of them, sending them to college, surviving the winters and waiting for the summers on the coast.

Henry was the first to marry. It seemed natural. He was the oldest. The year was nineteen and forty-two. Married a nice girl, Riva Botstein, by name. From Bangor. They met after he graduated from Bowdoin. Before the wedding, I gave Old Man Botstein a case of that Canadian whiskey—my last one from a strategic acquisition many years before. I am proud of myself for that. But the night before we were to leave for Bangor, I developed the worst headache I ever had. I was beside myself in pain. Somehow, I managed to get to the wedding. I lasted through the ceremony, but I had to leave in the middle of dinner. It was awful. I was fifty-three, getting up there a bit, but not so old. It was my first encounter with ill health.

Things did not get better. They got worse. The headaches continued, and my vision blurred. I got so I was afraid to drive at night. The local doctor put it down to nerves. The U.S. was at war in Europe and the Far East, and it was a dark period for all Americans. But that did not seem right to me. I had lived through World War I, prohibition, and the depression, and so I did not think my nerves were bad. Then I had a convulsion. Mary said that one night after dinner she found me shaking on the floor. In a panic she called our doctor, who came by and gave me an injection for my nerves. It didn't help. Nothing helped. A month later I had another attack. The doctor thought I might have some form of epilepsy and gave me a prescription for Phenobarbital for the seizures. It didn't seem to help much. Was there nothing to be done? Finally, we went to Boston to see a famous neurologist. He did what he called a neurological exam and got my blood counts. At the end—we stayed three days—he said I was not crazy, that it was not all "in my head." I had some disease, but it was not clear what. He gave me a prescription to calm me and asked me to come back in six months.

That turned out to be impossible. The convulsions became more frequent. I had constant diarrhea. I would vomit after meals. One night I had a convulsion. When I stopped shaking, I stopped breathing too. The year was nineteen and forty-three.

Of course, I never knew the Hiram Markham who is missing. He was named for me since he was born the next year. I have no idea if he has Alzheimer's, but he was a numbers guy like me. Runs in the family. As a youngster, Henry was good as well.

Alzheimer's, my foot, I suspicion something bad has happened to him.

IV

Mary Coggin Markham

My husband Hiram was a wonderful husband. Goodness, we had known each other forever. The Jewish community in Lewiston was small. We grew up together. He had already been here a few years before I met him. He was shy and kept to himself at first. But eventually he came out of his shell. He was not a plodder—conscientious, yes, but a plodder, no. I always found him very gentle, but it is true he had a temper. He was not mercurial, but there were times . . . I heard stories about some of the fights he got into, but they were in his past.

He was surely inventive. He got the job done, whatever it was, but always with a twist. In high school we were only friends. We did not date. We never even held hands. I think it was his shyness that kept romance from developing. He might have been self-conscious because he had no family but the Lovetts. I never asked him, but I think he felt himself very much alone and had only himself to rely on. He went off to the University of Maine, and my family, remember the year was nineteen and eight, sent me to Boston. I lived with Aunt Sarah and Uncle Joe and attended Boston University. An English major I was.

We would see each other during vacations
and summers. Each year he seemed a little more
sure of himself, and one night he asked me to
the movies. Walking back, he kissed me. It was
a tentative peck on the lips, not more. But in
my mind, I am ashamed to admit this even now,
but in my mind it sealed things. I sensed where
my future was. I am giving you this background
about his mild nature and his, I guess I would
say, deportment because I want you to know
that he was a good man and we were very happy
together.

Which does not mean that everything he did
was good. I have read what he wrote, and I want
to offer, not a corrective, but an addition. Let me
preface it by saying again that he was a good man,
but, well, he, I do not know any other word for it,
he "sinned." What he did was not right. In fact
in was horrible. I do not know what came over
him—or me—in May of nineteen and twenty-five.

It was prohibition then and before the stock
market crash. The hardware store was doing
well, and more and more my father was slowing
down and relying on Hiram to take over. He had
a sharp mind and an eye for business. One day
a truck pulled up. On the cab was detailed Mario
Marino and Sons, Hardware Supplies, Boston,
Massachusetts. We had our regular jobbers.
These were people we had never heard of. It was
late afternoon, and my father had already gone,
leaving the store to the two of us. In walked Mario
and his partner, a man named Levy. One thing
led to another, and the three of them went back to
the office to chat. A little while latter Mario went
out to the truck, returned with a briefcase, and
closed the office door behind him. Oh, perhaps

twenty minutes later Hiram came out and told me that what they were offering was not nails and drill bits but Canadian whiskey, real Canadian whiskey. They had crossed the boarder north of us and were making their way south selling what they could. Seems they talked for a bit, and Hiram had asked to taste the booze. To oblige him Mario had gone out to the truck and returned with the briefcase.

About then I went home to relieve my mother, who was tending Henry and his sisters, and make dinner. The rest of what I am going to tell you only came out by degrees. We had no secrets, Hiram and I. I was his deep, deep confidant. His confessor. In truth as you will see, I was more than his confessor, I was his accomplice.

They had a few drinks, and my husband suggested that they pull the truck round back to the loading dock. They opened up the back. Hiram said it was packed half full with cases of whiskey exactly as they had promised. They went back to the office, continued to drink, and began to negotiate. In fact Mario and the Levy fellow were very much in their cups, and Hiram somehow was able to stay well behind them. He was hardly tipsy, he told me later. Mario was slumped over, his head planted firmly in the in-box on my father's desk. Levy's head gyrated and wobbled.

My husband walked out front and locked up the store. He said to Levy that he wanted to show him around a bit. As Levy staggered down the tool isle, oh God, I can hardly tell it, my husband picked up a hammer and hit him in the back of the skull I am not sure how many times. He went back, found Mario still slumped over, and dispatched him as well. He dragged both bodies to the truck, took the keys from Mario's pocket, and locked them in the back.

Hiram called and said he had to go to the beach house on business. At the time I remember thinking, *What? On a Tuesday evening?* He said he had to store some things. I figured he had bought some whiskey and was going to keep it down there out of sight. He explained he would be gone a few days. I could not figure out why it would take so long. When I objected, he told me to be calm; we could talk about it later. Seems he drove the truck down to the shore, parked it out of sight in the old stable, and dragged the bodies to the boat or perhaps he used the wheelbarrow. He loaded on some brick we were going to use to edge the flowerbeds and went out without his running lights. He dumped the brick into two traps, tied each body by a leg to a trap, and pushed them overboard far out in the bay. Even today, separated by so many years, it is hard to express how horrible this event, this aberration in his character, was. And mine as well. How sorry I am.

He told me that he came back in, saved half the whiskey in the stable for us, and loaded the rest onto the lobster boat. He worked his way down the coast, hugging the shore, again without his running lights, heading for Boston. There he tried to sell the contraband. A bunch of toughs beat him up on a wharf. They bloodied his face, left a gash over his eye and broke his arm. They unloaded the whiskey, started the boat's engine, put him at the helm, and jumped off.

Somehow, he made his way back up the coast and called me. For the life of me, I cannot recall exactly how long he was gone. It must have been several days. My parents took the children, and I went to get him. When I found him sitting in the kitchen, I screamed. He sat there dazed, almost trance-like. He was an awful sight, blood on his face and in his hair, the gash and his shirt matted to his chest with blood. I cleaned him and painted his wounds with mercurochrome. He winced as I slipped his left arm out of his shirt. "Hiram, what have you done?" I said. When he told me, I wept for those unfortunate men. I wept for Hiram and myself. Our life would never be the same. It would always hang over us, even if we escaped detection. Later as I thought about it, I realized there had been more to his early brawls than youthful disagreements. There must have been a deeply sinister pool of evil in him that occasionally seeped out. Thank God, that was the one and only time I ever saw it.

There was still the question of the truck. I fed him tea and toast with jam, and he slept a few hours. He went out to the truck, which was still in the stable, and with his one good hand sanded off the logo, filed off the serial number, and removed the license plates. Honestly, I do not know how he managed. He rested, and that night I followed him up the coast. In a deserted spot he rolled it off a cliff into the sea. We headed back to Lewiston. When we got to the doctor's the next morning, I explained that he was cleaning the gutters at our beach house and had fallen off the roof. Lucky he was not killed, the doctor had said. I held my tongue.

I have never told anyone this story. It is so shameful, but I have to say something. It has been festering inside me, and I could not let it go unnoted. No death should go unnoted. And when I read what Hiram wrote, I felt obliged to complete the record. Thank God, no harm can come of it now.

Before and after that week in May of nineteen and twenty-five, it was good living with him. He always treated me well, never raised a hand or even his voice. There was simply something inside him, I do not know what, some compulsion toward the violent that I saw only that one time. Perhaps it is in the bloodline of that family. And the sad part is he died so young. Fifty-four is much too young.

Out of the blue, he started to have headaches. They persisted and got worse and worse. Eventually they became incapacitating, and he began to have convulsions. Our doctor said it was epilepsy, but when he couldn't provide poor Hiram with any relief, we went down to Boston, to Massachusetts General Hospital. They could not help him either. They had no diagnosis. I wondered if it was diabetes. He used so much sugar in his coffee. He always had to have things sweet. His cereal, jam on his toast. He never seemed to get enough. I raised it. He hushed me, but I raised it. He was always a private man. Diabetes turns out not to have been the problem. The doctor said that his blood and urine were fine for sugar. He died soon after Henry's wedding. The funny thing is that I had a headache or two at the same time, nothing like his, but all the same, they were there. Probably only a simple coincidence. Whatever poor Hiram had, it was not contagious.

Our son Henry named his first son for him, young Hiram, and of course you now know that young Hiram has disappeared. We are not a religious family, but I was glad to see the name preserved. I got to know young Hiram well—he was twenty when I died. I did not see him graduate from Harvard, but I thought that it was quite a change—my living with my aunt and uncle and going to Boston University, and his living in Adams House and going to Harvard. My Hiram and Henry were smart, but not like that young whippersnapper. There was nothing he did not know or understand.

It breaks my heart to know he's missing. Maybe it is Alzheimer's as they say. My husband had a neurological problem, and maybe young Hiram's problem is related. So it is possible. I worry. His grandfather, my husband, did not do so well, and we do not yet know young Hiram's fate.

I have been luckier, maybe because I carry no Markham blood or because I am a woman. Except for that terrible time with the Canadian whiskey and the truck, I have lived a quiet life. I remember when there were no cars to speak of. I used a crystal set, then a radio, a black and white T.V., and color. I saw propeller planes and jets, then Sputnik. Two world wars, Korea. And what matters most is my family, living in Lewiston, and the house on the bay. Whatever happens to Hiram, he has Penny, his twin sons, and his daughter Henrietta to carry on.

V

Henry Markham

My father Hiram was an evil man, a harsh man. He clenched his iron fist beneath a glove of civility. You hear it said when men speak of rough justice that some ask no quarter and grant none. With my father it was different. He asked for mercy, understanding, love, but he was cold as stone. He had no scruples. One day Canadian whiskey began to appear in our lives. It was prohibition, and my father had an ample supply, which he used to buy favors and to facilitate his life. I had no idea who turned on the tap. How could I? I must have been about eleven. It was years later that I realized that the truck the troopers found dumped in Restacott Bay and my father's booze were connected. You would have thought it enough to be given an opportunity in this country, to have relatives take him in, change his name, spruce him up, and set him on a proper course. They never found the driver or his assistant, but I am certain as the sunrise that my father disposed of them just as he did the truck.

I was the oldest, but he scarcely paid attention to me. I raised myself. In part he was preoccupied with the store and my mother, though I believe he had another life. He would disappear for a day or two, and no one would comment. My mother would run the store and ignore his odd behavior. Whether it was gambling or women or booze, or something more sinister, perhaps satanic, we never found out. One day I realized why he kept the old horse stable locked. That was where the cache was. He banked from the stable at the summerhouse.

The only thing he ever did for me was take me out on the bay in the lobster boat. He and I would fool with a few traps and maybe bring home dinner. We were long past the idea of lobster being *treif*, even in the twenties. It is true, he introduced me to lobstering. I came to love it, an addiction was the way my father phrased it. I purposely chose Bowdoin so that I could be close. I would steal away whenever I could to set a line of traps or retrieve the catch. What I sold kept me in pocket money, which I used to visit the girls when I felt the need. And summers I lobstered full time. The tourists always came, and I could sell everything I caught. It hardly mattered that I was getting a liberal education. My parents were very proud of that, but I was not a contemplative type. I was, at heart, a tradesman. At first Riva, who later became my wife, didn't know what to make of this.

It is odd that she did not understand how I wanted to live my life. We met while she was still at Tufts. I was just starting out full-time in the lobster business. Each summer the Botstein clan—they were from Bangor—headed south and rented a place near us. One day she happened by my roadside stand. It was late and I had only a few pathetic, chicken lobsters left. Six was what she wanted. "Come back tomorrow in the afternoon," I said. "I'll save some choice ones for you." And that's how the relationship began. It was an oddity in her eyes that a Jewish guy from Lewiston, an English major, ran a lobster business. I fascinated her. And soon that summer she was going out with me, setting the traps, hauling in the catch. For her this was a frolic, a souvenir of summer. For me it was my livelihood. We wrote during the winter, and I even went down once when she had a few days off at Washington's Birthday and took her to dinner. As soon as Riva arrived the next summer, she looked me up. We both knew that she was not the outdoor type, but we had a very strong animal attraction. By now I was getting myself established in the lobster business. I had scraped together enough to buy a new boat. I called my product Markham's Maine Pride Lobsters. We married a few years later.

There is a story behind how I came to own the place on the coast. Normally, when people do something wrong, if they own up to it at all, they say that they did such and such and are not proud of it, but they did it. I guess I'm different because I'm proud of my ingenuity. When it hit me that I was to be married, I suddenly realized I had to own the property on the bay myself. My parents could come down and visit, but it had to be mine. I would make my life there. I needed to be able to support a family. Slowly I worked through a plan. I went through a lot of ideas. A boating accident or a car crash. A fall. An accidental drowning. A robbery at the store in Lewiston. I needed a way to ease my father out of the picture. I even imagined garroting him and linking it to the hijacked load of Canadian whiskey. An overdue vendetta killing.

In the end, I settled for something a little more subtle and harder to detect. I remembered my father's sweet tooth and my mother's indifference to sugar. With that bit of knowledge everything fell in place. I laced the sugar in my Mother's kitchens in Lewiston and at the house on the bay with arsenic. I knew it would be ten to one. My father would be stricken and my mother hardly affected. I have to say, and I admit to a little pride here, it worked very smoothly—better than I expected. When it was over, my mother was well taken care of with the store in Lewiston, and so I proposed a very inexpensive buy-out. I was her son and newly married. The house at the shore is where her grandchildren would live. Of course, she agreed. I didn't miss my father.

I have never told this story before. Even Riva knew nothing of my deed. I have never breathed a word to anyone. But it is safe to tell the story now. I am safe beyond the grave. And it is important if we are to consider my son Hiram's disappearance. There is some flicker of greed and evil that runs through our family. My grandfather Dov-Ber in the old country had it, and my father the elder Chaim Markstein/Hiram Markham had it. I believe my son Hiram had it. The consequence is that there may be some ugly aspect of Hiram's character that led to his disappearance. And it's been so long since anyone has heard from him that I'm sure he's dead. It is impossible for me to know, but he might have been the victim of a vendetta killing or perhaps he died committing some heinous crime. I have no way of knowing. But I do not think he died a natural death. There is something in the blood of our family that pushes us beyond normal boundaries.

There was no denying my son's gifts. Like his namesake, there was a chilling clarity in his vision of the world—and a knack for exploiting opportunity. He was almost a prodigy. From an early age there was no doubt about his intelligence. Riva and I even considered sending him off to boarding school, but he would have none of it. He loved the water and the boats too much. And who was I to dispute him? There was no doubt in my mind that Harvard would accept him. After all, how many sons of Jewish lobsterman from Maine have perfect SATs? I worried a bit about his being Jewish since the quotas were just lifting in the Ivies. But off he went. And he acquitted himself well.

In my opinion, the only blemish on his record occurred up here on the water. I say "in my opinion," but because most people saw it differently. It has to do with the Wilma Donegal woman. They were hot and heavy as young people are. He was home from college for the summer. She was a nice young thing, as I remember. Pretty and perky. I understand why he liked her. Then one day she just disappeared. Of course, the police talked to Hiram since they were spending so much time together. At first they didn't suspect him; they thought perhaps he could help with some leads. He knew nothing or so he said. He had no idea where she had gone or why. And there was nothing to tie him to her disappearance. Perhaps later they became suspicious, but they had nothing to go on. In the fall he went back to college in Boston. They knew where he was if they needed him. She had simply vanished without a trace. At the time I had this strange vision, a recollection of a movie I had seen. A crocodile slid quietly from the bank of an African river into the water and was never missed. Wilma Donegal seemed to slip away. I have no evidence either way. But I'm a pretty good judge of human nature, and I've already told you about our bloodlines.

This is only speculation, but if I am right about Wilma's disappearance, then we have evidence of his character and reason to suspect he died because of some treachery on his part. One of the problems with being dead is that you can no longer act in the world. You are emasculated. The other is that you do not have rapid access to the latest information. We have to wait for happenings to trickle over. And sometimes they don't make it. Wilma is an example. I'll bet anything—I was about to say I'd stake my life on it, but then there's no collateral in that—that she's dead and died a wrongful death. But until we find her remains or understand why we can't, we will be, like everyone else, in the dark.

VI

Riva Botstein Markham

Grandma Riva and I are sitting at Cafe Spetses in Harvard Square having tea. There is quite a bit of noise from a bunch of soccer fans across the room watching a game on a flat panel T.V., which is one reason I don't come here too often. We are visiting after her ophthalmology checkup. She likes her ophthalmologist in Boston—it gives her an excuse to come down and shop and visit the museums. She is glad to join me to talk about my father's disappearance. Uncle George has brought her down from Lewiston. She moved there from the coast to a retirement community near Aunt Cindy and him a few years ago. He's coming for her in an hour, so I put the question directly to her, "What do you think happened to Daddy?"

"The truth is, Henrietta, I don't know that I have a lot to contribute, but I'll try to do my best. At my age it is hard to remember details. I'm going to start back some. To begin with your Grandfather Henry was a wonderful person. Don't look at me that way, Darling. Just be a little patient. I've been lonely without my Henry. He died so many years ago. I don't know exactly.

It's hard to keep track. You're a senior in college now, and your parents named you after him. The one who died too young was Hiram, Chaim really, your great grandfather. Just a little after we were married—he had these horrible stomach pains. He died a wretched death. The doctors were at a loss to help him. He was young, fifty-four, even for that day. Your father was named for him. Well, almost—he was named for his adopted name, Hiram.

"Of all the family, they were most alike, your father and your great grandfather. Both were very smart. Oh, Darling, with your father I don't know whether to say 'is' or 'was' very smart. And I'd like to add they were both a little distant. By distant I don't mean that they were not polite or didn't make a good impression. They did. Yet both had the same distracted way about them. They always seemed preoccupied. When you looked to them for something, you encountered a vagueness as if they were in the middle of a long string of calculations and hadn't quite finished. Their manner sent signals not to disturb them as if they would lose the result and have to start over again. With both of them, you never knew exactly what was going on in those brains of theirs.

"No one in the Markstein/Markham family had any Jewish learning. One reason we let your father and your mother Penelope marry is that by the time I came to the family, Henry was, I was about to say Jewish in name only, but of course Henry Markham is not a Jewish name, at least not one that you would normally think of as Jewish. Well, your father met your mother in Boston and that was that. Not that I objected. She has been a good daughter-in-law to me. Much more attentive than your father really, but after all, isn't that the way of women? I never met the Lovetts—by the time I came to the family they were dead—but I don't think they, and certainly not your great grandfather, had much Jewish learning.

"They gave up the mystery when Chaim became Hiram. I kept thinking when I met your great grandfather he was going to offer me a whiskey—I had already heard about it from your grandfather Henry. Of course, as you already know, he had plenty of Canadian rye from some mysterious source. We all knew something was afoot. We just didn't know what. What I mean when I say forfeited the mystery is that in the family they could have called him Hy or Chai. Darling, you know the word *chai* in Hebrew means 'life' and more loosely 'luck.' It might have brought them more luck and less intrigue. There is another type of mystery around your father. I'm being honest. You are old enough to know these things. No one ever mentioned they believed your father was responsible for the missing Donegal girl, though at times I wondered. I know he's my son, but I am being brutally honest with you. I mean no one, but it is one thing not to mention and another not to think. The family could have used a little luck. Henry's father died so young. A *chai* might have helped him live. Oh, dear God, and your brothers. There is no sense pulling any punches. Enough said.

"And now my son's gone missing. You know no one ever tells me anything. If you're old and on your own, you pretty much have to rely on visits from family and T.V. The local tom-toms of the coffee shop and ladies lunches hardly exist for me now. I worry about independence. I don't know how much longer your father and your Uncle George are going to let me live alone or keep my license. Anyway, I don't go many places, and about December first I stop driving. The last thing I want to happen is that I'll be out and break down in the cold and freeze to death before they find me.

"I'll tell you one thing though—it's not Alzheimer's. It doesn't run in the family, and you know when your father comes to Lewiston to visit, I'll give him a list of things to get for me—I like the Revlon face products and Glide better than regular dental floss. He never writes anything down and never forgets. He'd be back in no time with everything, just like that. I don't care what it was or where he had to go, he found it and brought it back. So you can forget Alzheimer's. Besides, he's your father. You know this as well as I do. Anyone who can do The *Times* crossword puzzle the way he can, sometimes all the way through Saturday, does not have Alzheimer's.

"Don't think me loony, but I favor conspiracy. Really. I know you're going to find this hard to believe, but when I was growing up in Maine, the Klan was active. There weren't many Jews back then even in Lewiston or Portland or Bangor where I'm from. Well, I was very young in the twenties, but I can still remember the stories about your great grandfather Hiram buying a shotgun and shells. He kept it loaded, your great grandmother Mary said, and locked away in a glass-fronted cabinet in the hall. He called it his American Torah. One day when I asked him what that meant, he said, 'It is my American Torah because it represents the law, my just-in-case law.' Of course, nothing ever came of it, not in any of those cities. Compared to the Catholics we were invisible. Who would swat a housefly when the deer flies were so thick?

"Strange bird, my father-in-law. As I look back on it, I was lucky. As I said, strange he was, Chaim Markstein. It was always 'Hiram.' But I come from a traditional background, so I always thought of him as Chaim. As I sized him up, he always had a glint of *shtetl* madness in his eyes. And my son, your father, well, I love him, but he is hardly Mr. Rotarian. For a Markham, my Henry was as normal as they come. The only one.

"Now the fact that your father is strange doesn't mean he has Alzheimer's and simply walked away. But it could mean he was into something private or primitive or occult. Voodoo, tarot readings with strangle rituals, even a gambling debt. I wouldn't put any of that past your father. But realistically speaking, Maine is not Las Vegas or the South Bronx. There is no opportunity for such deep mischief, or at least I don't think there is. In Maine satanic rites are something you read about. Nothing happens here. I guess, deep down, I do not believe anyone abducted and killed him. That sounds too much like what you see on T.V. So in my book, he is either on the run or has met an unhappy end for a personal involvement we cannot imagine. No, Darling, I do not believe he killed himself in some out-of-the-way place. He loved life too much. I don't think he had any debt to speak of.

"What I believe is that his odd personality got him into trouble. Someone misunderstood his reclusive nature and figured he was guilty of some far-fetched thing like rape or murder or something totally unfounded. That person or persons kidnapped him, took him out of state to some place with lots of land and even fewer people than there are in Maine and did him in. Oh, I hate to think of it. To have a child die before you is a terrible thing. This is not a pretty picture, is it? But on the other hand it makes more sense to me than any other explanation.

"Well, Child, what do you think? I know you're going to tell me that you are only a college student and don't have any idea, but please tell me."

"Honestly, Grandma, I want to hear from you. I'll tell you later."

"There is not much more to say. You come from an odd family. Except for my Henry, so many of your family are strange. First there was Chaim. Actually, as he told me in confidence one day, even his father in the old country got into some sort of trouble that cost him his life. I don't know what, but there it is. So there is your great, great grandfather, your great grandfather, maybe your father and Wilma Donegal, and, I hate to say it, because nothing has happened yet, maybe your twin brothers. Only my Henry was an innocent. I believe that with two of them, your brothers, their risk will be doubled. There will be no double *chai* for them. But you, my child, are different. When I look into your beautiful face, I know you have escaped this mark of Cain.

"My Dear, I have gone on long enough. I'm an old woman, but I know when to shut up. That's all I know about your father. When you are back in Maine to visit, come by. Most of my contemporaries are gone or debilitated. All I have is my reading and occasional visits from family."

"I will, Grandma, I promise. It is all so unclear. I have no idea where he is or what happened. If I have some flash of insight that can help find him, I'll talk to Mom and we'll go to the police. I don't even know where to begin to look. Suppose something bad did happen, as you suggest, and he's been kidnapped. Well, unless they send a ransom note, we don't have a clue how to search for him. He could be anywhere. There is no way to make sense of this yet. We need more information."

"Henrietta, I worry so, and I am so powerless. There is nothing I can do. Darling, this has worn me out. Please call your Uncle George and ask him to come pick me up."

VII

Wilma Donegal

Oh, God, Hiram, I never lived my life because of you. I never married or had children, never finished my schooling. I was a good student, Sister said so. I could have gone to college, made something of myself, not like the others in my family. I gave myself to you. You were the only one. You said you loved me. You seemed so kind and gentle. I never thought you had deceit in you. You kissed my lips softly as if it were a sacred act. Your hand felt like a feather on my cheek. What came over you? I didn't resist. I was glad. You kissed me and later we made love. It was my first time. My only time. How wonderful it was. My body felt electric. You went to wash up, and when you came back, I remember clearly, I was lying on my side. I felt so grand in your presence. I can still feel your hands on my neck and back. Your touch was light—silky and robust. I was half asleep when you said, "Don't move. I want to remember you this way forever." Suddenly, I felt a burning on the left between my ribs. It was like a poker there. In my last instant of life as the stab pierced my heart and blood surged through my chest, I remember thinking, *This is what Christ's wounds must have felt like, the stigmata.*

I never imagined after death I would still suffer pain each instant. I do not know if this is hell, but I thought everything would go blank and there would be nothing. Instead, I replay that instant when I trusted you, gave you my heart and my virginity, and in return you took my life. Living stopped when you stabbed me. I didn't expect that those last minutes would go on and on forever as punishment. Why am I punished for trusting you? It felt like a nail driven between my ribs and into my heart. I never saw what you used to violate me. I imagine it was something like an ice pick. Now I think, *How odd that an instrument designed for ice has caused such burning in my side.* I am forever in this murky darkness. Its chill goes through me like a cutting wind. It is the worst cold imaginable. My only warmth radiates from my wound. Every instant I feel the spot between my ribs where you slipped the ice pick on its way to my heart.

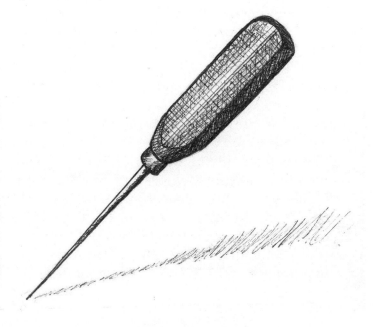

My God, you must have planned my death carefully, waiting for a weekend when your parents went to Boston. How else could there be an ice pick or a knife in the bedroom? You moved so deftly to snuff out my life. And I loved you. When did you first know that you would use my body twice for different lurid pleasures? I had imagined we made love that night. Now I know you raped me just as surely as if you had taken me by force. How could I have been so wrong about you? Your smile was warm and your manner always gentle. Home that summer from college, you took me to the beach to walk. I still remember how the sandpipers would skit about as we walked toward the lighthouse in the surf, the water rolling in and pushing us further up the beach and then sucking at our feet.

You were always tender when you touched me. I asked you what would make you happy and you said that you would love to watch me bake a blueberry pie. We made a day of it, first bringing back what seemed like gallons of berries in plastic pails and washing them in your kitchen sink. While I prepared the dough and rolled it out, you buttered corn and wrapped the ears in silver foil for the grill. We drank bourbon and ginger ale, and after supper I cut you a wedge of pie. You said, I will never forget how beautiful it sounded, "Tonight on Parnassus the gods do not dine as well as we do, Aphrodite. Like her, Wilma, you are born of the sea foam." I thought you spoke so well and knew so much. I was eighteen, just eighteen years old. I knew nothing.

When you began to explore my body, I let you. I welcomed you. I was not ready to lose my virginity, but I thought, *Here is a man I can trust who truly loves me.* I greeted you joyously with my body. How bitter it is to think that I gave my heart to you to stab, a final pleasure for your perverted mind.

Now I am in Limbo, waiting. The news of your death pleased me. I was thrilled to hear how you died. You must have gasped for breath and choked as the salt water filled your lungs. They caged you like the animal you are. In your last instant you must have pushed with all your strength against the slats to break free. You monster, you deserved to suffer. You snuffed out my life before I had one.

I have only one regret about your death— that you did not suffer more. They should have set the gasoline afire and let you burn some. Just enough to take your skin off. They should have salted you and left you in the sun a day, then loaded you on the lobster boat. There is no place in hell hot enough for a murderer like you. Maybe they should have opened the trap before they took you out and let the dogs gnaw you. They should have taken pliers to your privates.

There is no going back. I have lost my life. An innocent has lost her life. I float in the cold depths while I burn in pain. One day I hope to find you. I must earn my redemption with a retributive strike. I did not learn this in my catechism classes. Rough justice is what one learns from life. I am an innocent no longer. I am free, and you are caged by your sin. My dream is to come across you one day, my love, strangle you and watch your eyes bug out.

VIII

George Markham

I am Hiram's younger brother, George. His only brother. His only sibling. I am also his lawyer. I don't see him very often since we live up here in Lewiston, and he and Penny are down on the coast. I'm going to leave the most important thing for last. At least, that's the way I look at it. His disappearance may be out of guilt. It's only speculation, but I think one issue may be key.

I want to get some other possibilities out of the way first. I do not think, no, I am certain my brother did not suffer from Alzheimer's. I talked to him once a week, at least, and there is no way he had Alzheimer's, period. No one with Alzheimer's could have remembered the things he did, down to the smallest detail, like the color of Miss Macpherson's eyes—our second grade teacher—or all the battles of the Civil War. Whatever happened to my brother, pure and simple, it was not Alzheimer's. I don't have a theory. But he had all his marbles, of that I'm certain. Now epilepsy is another matter. That's what our grandfather, the first Hiram Markham, died from. And, who knows, he might have had a seizure while walking in the woods, and they just haven't found him.

I want to suggest another possibility. He might have wanted to get lost. Maybe he had had enough of his two imbecile sons and the lobster business. He practically ran a sheltered workshop for them. I don't know how two people like Hiram and Penny could have spawned them. They are both so bright. So maybe he just went AWOL, deliberately went off the grid, decided to lead a counterculture life in some quiet place. He could figure anything out. He was a great planner. I'm guessing he might have squirreled away a few dollars. He might have withdrawn his money and taken a plane to almost anywhere. It would not be out of character.

There may be no mystery at all. Perhaps he wanted one last crack at something different before he died. Or maybe he went to prepare for death—like Ambrose Bierce going to Mexico. Besides the idiot twins, there is his daughter Henrietta. She is a piece of work. Super bright like her father and just as stubborn and sure of herself. Maybe he got tired listening to her parse the world. Like him she went to Harvard. Actually, she's a senior this year. Haaarvard.

The only reason I'm dismissing my idea of a disappearing stunt is his wife Penny. They loved each other as far as I can tell. It wasn't always easy living with Hiram, but she is a trouper. She came as close as anybody keeping up with him. I don't think he would have left her. No, if he had wanted to make an escape, he would have taken her. Besides, if he wanted to leave, why not just rent an R.V. and go, or buy two tickets to Paris? There wouldn't have to be any secrecy. He didn't have to take the phone calls or return emails. He could have ignored all of it. There was no need for drama. Hiram wasn't like that.

We also have to consider that he is up to something more sinister or is running from a crime. He had the mind for perfect crimes. Who knows—maybe there is a Madoff backstory of some sort, and he's cashing out and running? This doesn't feel likely. Other than surreptitious trips to Vegas, there's nothing that I know of. Vegas, maybe he just wanted some peace and to focus on poker tournaments. I'm sure if he wanted, he could support himself that way, and handsomely too.

When it comes to my brother's activities, there can be no end to conjecture. He was protean in his talents and his interests. And he had great powers of concentration. He may have planned an exit so slick we'll never find him. In my opinion, the only one who could possibly put this all together is his daughter Henrietta. She's got the brains to figure it out. You almost want to accuse those knucklehead twins of something nefarious—they never liked their father. But, I don't think so. For one thing, the two of them together are barely smart enough to get the traps out and bring in the catch. They might be able to mastermind a trip to Boston, but that's about as far as it goes.

I understand my brother could be maddening. When he was concentrating, which in the last ten years seemed more and more often, he would freeze you out. He focused on what was before him and nothing else. The fact that he and the boys shared the business that our Dad left them must not have made things any easier. I'll tell you,

I'm glad that I got out. It may not be so glorious or so interesting being a small town lawyer in Lewiston, but it's a hell of a lot better than being out on the bay winter and summer with a couple of dunces. That's no kind of life. Maybe Hiram couldn't stand it and offed himself. It wouldn't be the first time someone had done that. If he did, he'd do it in a quiet fashion. Disappearing like that would not be out of character. I blow hot and cold on this. I'm curious to know what happened, but if he is on the lam or took his life in some private, ingenious way, well, more power to him. If he had wanted us to know, he would have left a note or contact information.

I guess the other thing to consider is a crime. Could someone have killed him for . . . for what? As I understand it, there's nothing missing. His car's where it always is. To the best of my knowledge his bank accounts are all intact. Penny has told me of nothing missing. His credit cards have not been used. How much money could he have had with him? Surely, knowing Hiram, no more than a few hundred dollars— unless he was getting ready to go to Vegas. In truth, he could be there right now, just taking a breather from Maine.

Of course, there is always the insurance, but Penny's the beneficiary of it all. So that's a non-starter. As for his will, again, everything goes to Penny. So money's not a motive for a crime. Yet there could be collusion. He disappears, she collects the insurance, and they meet up in their private version of Shangri-La. It's been done before. They are clever enough, those two.

Do others have a score to settle? I wouldn't have thought so, not locally. He was just a loner. People took very little notice of him and he of them. Perhaps he offended someone in a way I can't imagine. That's always possible. But who? There is one possibility. Maybe he's got a debt in Vegas that he can't pay. He always seemed so prudent, almost dispassionate about his gambling. But again it's possible. Maybe he is a very cool customer who isn't showing his personal cards at all. That doesn't feel right to me, but people do have a way of hiding what they don't want you to see.

All of this doesn't add up to more than speculation. We need more facts. Until some clue turns up, we're guessing.

Do I miss him? Well, yes and no. As I mentioned, we talked by phone a lot, and you might call us close in that we know each other's affairs. But we aren't emotionally close. No one except maybe Penny is really close to him. It doesn't mean I don't like him, but time and life take us all in different directions. Mine's been straightforward. My law practice, Cindy and the kids, now a new grandchild. Who could have believed it? A grandson. Sitting for him last night, I was simply overcome with joy, a sense that all is right with the world. Except for Hiram, that is. No, my life is simple. The usual list of things—getting the car inspected, the temple men's club, golf, in the summer anyway, hiring a new legal secretary. Hiram is on my mind, but really not that much.

This is where I would like my contribution to end. Here with only the facts I have presented and a little clarification. Yet there is one more thing too important to ignore. It's Wilma Donegal. I'm not sure most people today will even remember her. She would have been, I don't know, sixty-three, sixty-four now. Hiram had a crush on her, and they spent a lot of time together. They were what we now would call "a number." They were thick back then. It was odd. One day she simply disappeared. Vanished, just like that—out of South-Central Maine, for Christ's sake. No one vanishes from around here—and back then, everybody knew everybody. In fact no one at the time could remember the last time it happened. It was deeply odd to think of Wilma as a run-away or kidnapped and molested. Odd and sad.

What I couldn't get my arms around was Hiram. He seemed muted rather than distraught. Subdued. Not like someone who had lost the girl he could have married. I only raised the issue once with him, the rest is observation—the way he moved, his facial expressions, that he said almost nothing. I said something like, "I'm sure you are broken up about Wilma. I know you two were a couple." And he stared at me for an instant—it was a piercing stare—and then looked away. It was a stare that said, *Don't go there.* It was then I suspected that he knew more than he was saying or that he could even be the cause of her disappearance. I never raised the issue with him again, and after a few months, most everybody in town except her family let go of it. Which is natural.

My brother forgot nothing, nothing. I wonder if there is some foul play here. To state it plainly, I'd like to rethink my position. It is entirely possible that he took his life out of guilt. He held his own confidences as I say, but knowing him, he could have found something in some book that said, You will be guilty throughout eternity and your seed as well unless you offer up your life. I don't mean to sound melodramatic here, like a televangelist, but this is my intuition. I don't think we will never know, but I wanted to raise this possibility because it is important and no one else could know this.

IX

Penelope Standarian Markham

There is no other way to put it: my husband Hiram is an original. I knew this from the first. I was at Radcliffe and he at Harvard when we met. There was a tea dance, that's what they were called in those days, at Adams House, and that fall afternoon of my freshman year Heather and Rachel dragged me to it. I was a shy thing then, and the notion of putting myself on display horrified me. I would rather have stayed at home like my namesake weaving and unraveling an afghan each day, awaiting the appearance of an imagined lover, a prince charming steeped in the classics. But as it happened, I put on a plaid skirt and knee socks and the obligatory white blouse—I cringe as I think about how unsure and conventional I was—and went with them.

I found myself at a window standing next to a slight young man with sandy brown hair who was staring out at something. He was engrossed, oblivious to my presence. I was intrigued. Here was someone who wanted to be here even less than I. It came to me by degrees that if I were to find out who he was and what was preoccupying him, I would have to initiate a conversation. He was off somewhere and had not the slightest need to return. Little did I know then that Hiram would often be swallowed by his mind for long periods, emerging only when he was ready or biology called him to dinner or sleep or love.

I must have said something like, "Hi, what on earth is so interesting out there?" The vagueness in his face told me I had intruded, but he did not seem displeased. He pointed to an oak and said he was examining its leaves, which though dead continued to cling to its branches. He was estimating how many leaves it had.

"Why on earth do you want to know that?"

"Because if I can estimate that number and determine the average weight of a single dry leaf, which is not hard to do, then I can go to the Boston Common, and excluding the conifers and assuming to a first approximation that all large deciduous trees have the same number of leaves of some average size, I can estimate the weight of all the leaves there in the fall. Knowing that value, I can look up the caloric value of a leaf and estimate how much heat one could generate if all the leaves were collected and burned in a power plant."

This was thirty years before this kind of thinking became popular.

My first impulse was to excuse myself and slip away. I tried to imagine Odysseus coming home after twenty years to the other Penelope and announcing he was interested in "biomass"—I am not sure what term they used when I was in college, but that is what we would say today. Some instinct kept me there. I think what held me was the wild passion in his eyes. He needed to know this number, really needed to know. It was his odd way of making order in the world, and since I had no interest in finding the son of an investment banker from Darien, I stayed.

"Penelope," he said when I told him my name, "you don't hear that very often. Who encumbered you with such malfeasance?"

"I was not encumbered, as you put it." To peak his interest I added, "And neither was I christened. My father is a professor of classics. He is a pantheist."

Well, you get the idea, two odd balls at a tea dance at Adams House in October. It was less clear that we were made for each other than that we were, as again we would say today, the best available option for each other.

My life with Hiram has been good on the whole. There have been some disappointments— the twins are at the top of that list. I do not understand where they came from. It's true we lived a semirustic life. Hiram made his living in the family lobstering business, but there were books in the house and conversation. Interesting people came to dinner. None of that took. I got two leaden boys, honestly, not fit for more than ballast.

Henrietta was as unlike the twins as tripe and ribs. She came along later, after my father-in-law Henry died and the boys were almost teenagers. Naturally, she was of a different generation, but she is more the type of child I expected Hiram and I would have—bright, curious, and, to be honest, a little eccentric in the Markham way. We named her for her grandfather, of course, in the Jewish tradition. Today, that feels a quaint touch. My family was nothing, but in the eyes of most people that made us protestant, and Hiram, while

Jewish, was, like me, agnostic. Religion never entered into our lives, formally speaking, that is. Yet the children, and especially Henrietta, had a vague sense that they were Jewish. And for a time we joined a temple and sent her to religious school. I didn't object. I was puzzled.

Loneliness was a problem in the early years. The boys would be at school and Hiram off on the boat or fussing with gear. And I was stuck on a small spit of land alone. My nearest neighbor was my mother-in-law. Enough said. It wasn't until dinner that I had any adult conversation, and much of the day I had no conversation at all. Once the twins were in school, I applied for a part-time position as a school librarian in Fosterport. Finally, I had some adults to talk to, and I enjoyed the work. It was fun working with the children, though it made me wistful for the type of children I didn't have. The extra money was a help. We were not poor, but when the price of lobster fell, the income was welcome.

Then Henrietta came along—it was a surprise. I didn't think at forty-two I would be pregnant. Of course I was working and needed coverage, and so I enlisted Riva's help. We were very different people, my mother-in-law and I, but she had the time, in fact like me, too much time. She was alone after all. Sometimes she minded Henrietta, her husband's namesake, while I worked, and some nights she would cook, and the six of us would eat together. She is not a bad sort, but it was hard for me to fathom how she could have raised a man like Hiram. Then one day I realized Hiram raised himself.

I wouldn't say Hiram is moody, just distant at times. Then as now he often seemed preoccupied.

THE LOBSTERMAN'S DAUGHTER~69

At dinner he and little Henrietta would be off somewhere in their individual gaga lands, and the twins and Riva and I would be eating chicken and mashed potatoes. I marveled that the two of them managed to feed themselves given their meandering thoughts.

There was one thing about him I have never understood. He was not what you would call a fussy eater. Whatever we served he would eat without complaint and often without comment. I confess I never felt rewarded cooking for him. Or if we went into Boston to visit the museums or for a concert, he would eat the most prosaic of meals—chicken or pasta, or even meatloaf, if he could find it. There was only one thing he could not abide, and I never understood why. The first time I baked a blueberry pie, he said he could not tolerate those "berries of desecration," as he put it, and he excused himself from the table. He loved my peach pie and the custard pie I make. "Delicious" was his proclamation the first time he tasted my chocolate pie. But the blueberry set him off, and he never did explain why. I'm not sure he knew.

The weekend he disappeared I was away. My mother was alone in Burlington in assisted living. She had fallen and I had gone to tend to her. Long ago, I should have considered some option for her in Lewiston or someplace closer to us. My big concern was to get her through the crisis. It was strange that Evan and Hank didn't call me. I was furious when I found that my husband, their father, had disappeared, and they did not call. When I heard that they had called the police to say that he had Alzheimer's and wandered off, I went through the roof. I tried to correct the police report and the local news broadcasts, but no one was interested. They viewed that as a detail. The important thing was that he was missing.

My husband is eccentric, but he has all his faculties. In a way his sustained eccentricity is proof of that. I suspected foul play and told the police as much, but they said they had investigated and there were no signs of a struggle or anything unusual at the house or on the property. As far as they could determine, nothing was amiss with the boat or the lobster operation. I suppose it's possible that he could have simply left, gone off to explore some unsuspected passion, but that would have been out of character. He never would leave without telling me, not for days. For an afternoon, perhaps, or even overnight, but not for days. I don't think he left me and our life together. We have no secrets. Something bad has happened. I have no idea what. Or why. We have no money to speak of, and nothing, as far as I can tell, is missing.

When I got back, my attention focused on the twins. They seemed their usual selves. Perhaps a little sad or dispirited but that was all. Their very normalcy worried me. How could they be so calm, indifferent even? I asked the police to question them again. They declined. They said they had conducted extensive interviews and turned up nothing. They had no reason to "harass" them, the chief had said. I was stymied, nothing added up. I even wondered if a drifter or a crazy had killed him for the thrill of it. I decided against this possibility. There was no sign of struggle, no disruptions, no body. Still it is possible that a vagrant loaded poor Hiram's body into a pickup and went elsewhere to dispose of it. Yet this scenario feels far-fetched—as if the author of a play had introduced a magical element at the end to resolve the plot.

The solution felt closer to home, and the logical place to start was with Evan and Hank. I sat them down and interrogated them. He had vanished was all they could come up with. They said they had no idea what had happened. They had gone out to set some traps and when they returned, he was gone. There was nothing more to tell. The three had chatted briefly at the dock. They left, and when they got back in the middle of the afternoon, he was gone. They still hadn't seen him the next day, which, they remembered, was rainy. Hank said he was a little puzzled, but their father, he said, was always weird, so he was not surprised. Their story didn't wash with me. My gut told me there was something else. What was being left unsaid? Over the next few days, I cornered each separately. No luck. I learned nothing more. Look, these boys aren't that clever or manipulative. Surely, if there were something amiss, when I got each alone, I would have uncovered it. Nothing. I was, plain and simple, stuck.

They are so different from Hiram and Henrietta and me. It was that way from the beginning. I knew I was having twins. It seemed okay at first, but at seven months I had terrible cramping and bleeding. My ob did an emergency C-section. The boys shared a placenta and were small, small even for twenty-eight weeks. I worried. Hiram worried, but they pulled through. They were in the hospital for a month, but eventually we brought them home. They seemed normal enough. And in fact they are. It is only that they lack the gifts that came down from both sides of the family. They were slow in school, and even with tutoring, they struggled to keep up, not like Henrietta. I didn't know what to do. I couldn't cry, I couldn't grieve, and, soon, I couldn't hope. As the days rolled by and there was no word, I slowly realized that he would not return. I suspect he is dead. I fear some evil deed. But I have no proof, no leads, only an intuition. I have nowhere to start. Of course, I kept Henrietta in the loop, but she had been down in Cambridge when he disappeared. She was grieving deeply, more deeply than I was. I was distracted trying to figure what the final outcome would be. I was left in a purgatory. There was no way forward and no way back. Deep in my gut, I know the twins know more than they are telling, but how to get it out of them? Now I'm having a crazy thought: Hiram would have known what to do. He had abiding cleverness. I remain incredulous that the local authorities bought the Alzheimer's explanation of the twins and have no interest in further discussion.

X

Evan and Hank Markham

"My wife Alice says we should talk as little as possible about our father. This is Evan speaking. She is a legal secretary and should know. She says, 'Talk about anything else, lobstering, the volunteer fire department, even how we get it on, but stay away from Hiram. You will only be asking for trouble.' When Hank and I talk things over, we are like a tandem bike; we work together, always smoothly on everything. That is how it has to be if we are going to lobster together . . . . Of course, as twins, we did a lot of things together growing up. We both played end in high school. Thank God, there were two of them. It is not like quarterback or center. How would it have been if I was the quarterback and Hank was the center? That would not have been fair—he always would have gotten the ball first. So we talk things over. We work together now. Hank and I agree with Alice. It would be good not to say too much about the disappearance. There is not much to say anyway. Mom worked us over pretty good. She talked to us together, without Alice, for a long, long time. She was a great Mom growing up, and she was the same at first when we talked. Then she became kind of pushy."

"This is Hank talking. What surprised us is that I do not think she believed that Dad wandered away and that when we got back to the dock, he was gone. I say that because a few days later she talked to me alone and to Evan too. That never happened growing up. We had bunk beds, and every year she would change us. In the fourth grade I was on the bottom. Then in fifth grade I was on the top, which I liked because I had a better view of the outside. And I could kick Evan when I got down which was also a lot of fun. We did our lessons together and our chores together. When we got older, we would shovel out the cars together. That was in the winter when the snow would be bad. Everything, so that when she talked to us alone, I was bothered. She was upsetting the way the world was. She was very stern when we talked. She said things like, 'Tell me what happened to your father.' I would answer that I told you and Evan told you that he was gone when we got back. She would say, 'That cannot be. Your father would never leave without telling you or me. I want the truth.' I would say, 'That is the truth. That is what happened. He was not there when Evan and me got back.'"

"Hank is right. I have been listening, and the same thing happened to me. It is pretty rough when your Mom talks to you that way. At one point she said that she would not stand for any lying. I was hurt. I said, 'Mom, I would not lie to you, and Hank would not lie to you. I do not know what happened.' Mom said, 'I think you do and you are not telling me. I want some answers.' 'Mom, I already told you. We told you together, and Hank told you. He was not in the house when we got back. I would never lie to you. I am your son Evan. And Hank would not lie to you.' She threw her hands up in the air. You see that in the movies when a woman is upset. She said, 'Evan, you are not telling the truth. I know it and you know it. Tell me.' 'Mom, that is the story. Hank and I do not know where Dad is.' 'You better tell me. The two of you better tell me or there will be trouble.' No one wants to be on the bad side of their Mom, but Hank and I were not going to say anything. And this was before Alice gave us her advice. Hank's wife, Babe, was away. In high school everyone one called Mary Beth 'Babe,' because, oh, you know, she had great big knockers. She was away. Her company had sent a bunch of them to Philadelphia for special training. So she did not know about this and had no advice to give us.

"This is still Evan talking. I do not want Hank to take too much heat so I thought I would talk some more for a while. It was just the three of us that day. Alice was in Dad's house tidying up, and we were working outside. Like I say, it was a very friendly thing between Alice and me and Hank. We were not smoking or anything. We were sitting around talking and trying out ideas on each other. Dad was outside puttering. We just got to thinking. Of the three of us, Alice is the best thinker. She is good. And her advice is good. She said, 'The less said the better.' And so we are listening, Hank and me. Although no one called Alice 'Babe' in high school, she is very good looking too. Her advice, you remember, was to talk about anything but that Friday and the weekend. I know she did not mean anything. And here is what I mean. We have a lot of sex in our house. It is fun because we play dress up and sometimes good cop-bad cop. I am not going to listen to her on this one—about the sex thing. You could say that it is okay with her if I talk to my mother about sex because she said only Friday and the weekend were off limits. But I do not think that it is a good idea. I have never told anyone about our special closet. I do not even talk to Hank about such things, but now I guess he knows."

"It is okay, Evan. I am not going to tell anybody. You are like a brother to me. Well, that is a good thing. You are my brother, a twin, just like me. When we take our catch over to the collective, I am not going to tell that one. The guys would really like it, but I am not going to tell. In that way, things are good between Babe and me. That is all I am going to say on that score. I have only one thing to say about my Dad's disappearance. If Alice was here, I do not think that she would worry if I said this: I was surprised at how heavy Dad is."

"That is enough, Hank. If you want to talk, tell them about calling in Dad's disappearance or what Henrietta thought. She is a smart one, that Henrietta. You know she is in college down in Boston. At Harvard. You cannot get any better than that. Like Dad, that is where she went. Not Mom, she went to Radcliffe. What a funny sound that name has. Can you imagine jumping off a Radcliffe? That will be my joke when we go down to the cooperative together and Hank tells his brother joke. It will be a friendly competition. She made a special trip to come see us, Henrietta. Like Mom, she was kind of suspicious. 'He did not simply disappear,' she said. 'What happened?' We did not know what to say. We went back and forth. You know she is our little sister, but she is much, much younger. It is like we are not related. We were in junior high when she was born. We did not grow up together. So it is not like Mom. We do not have to be respectful of her questions."

"I will tell you this. She pushed Evan and me pretty hard. Sometimes she is not a nice person. It is not right when your sister, even if she is so much younger that she does not seem like your sister . . . when she called us rotten pieces of shit. It felt very bad. We never bothered her a bit. Where does she get off using language like that with us? She would not let up, not like Mom, who is basically nice. I have never seen Henrietta naked, but I bet she has tattoos somewhere on her body. I would like to see her naked. She lit into Evan and me. At one point she said, 'Where did you put Dad's body?' I was shocked. I did not know what to say. How could she ask a question like that? Then Evan jumped in."

"This is Evan again. 'How could you ask a question like that?' I said. 'We love Dad. He was not there when we got back.' 'Where was Alice then?' she asked. Why did she ask about Alice? 'I do not know,' I said. 'I was out on the boat with Hank. I guess she was at work or something.' Like Hank, the rotten piece of shit thing got to me. That is when I lost all respect for her. I said, 'Bitch, you go back down to that fancy Harvard of yours and hang out with all those fags. You cannot speak to family the way you are. We love Dad and hope they will find him soon.' You know what she said?"

"Let me tell them. This is Hank again. It was unbelievable. 'Yeah, right,' she said. 'The two of you are fucking idiots.' That was hurtful. We did not go to Harvard. But we are not idiots. We work for a living and pay our bills. We live a quiet life with our wives. What is her problem? Okay, it is true we were not at the top of our high school class, but we graduated. I still do not understand why the merchant marine would not have us. We graduated which is more than a lot of people do. That was when I lost it. She was not very nice in saying that. I know she was upset about Dad. Me and Evan were upset too. I said, 'You whore, you cannot speak of us that way.' I was going to slap her, but Evan grabbed my arm. 'You cannot hit your sister. It is not proper. Mom would not like it.' I said to myself, Evan is right."

"I am glad you agree, Hank. We should always agree. No one should drive up from Harvard and tell us we did something wrong and call us idiots. I said to her, 'Girl, you have a foul mouth. I am going to tell Mom.' She said she did not care, that I should 'Fuck off.' I was boiling over, and before Hank could grab my arm, I smacked her across the puss real good. 'That is what you get for talking ugly to your family.' Before I could hit her again, she was gone. We never did know what she thought about Dad wandering off the way we described it to her. We understood Mom. I did not like the way she behaved and I know Hank did not. But she is our Mom. But Henrietta is nothing. She came late. She is still in college. She has no right to ask these questions."

XI

Henrietta Markham

I have always loved my father deeply. I felt we had a special kinship, an unspoken bond because we viewed the world in the same eccentric way. Some days I thought we were closer than he and Mom. There is a special attraction between fathers and daughters, and we had it in spades. And now he is missing. My father is missing. He is a very gentle man. Learned too. And as I mentioned eccentric. He doesn't have a loose screw or any meanness. What he has is an intense curiosity—everything interests him—and an extraordinary ability to focus. To call Dad a lobsterman would be like calling Einstein a patent office clerk or Walt Whitman a typesetter. His mind is that unique. Of course everyone sees our similarities. Who could think either of us is like those idiot twins?

They still haven't found him, and I worry they won't. Or if they do, it will be horrible. I am looking forward to getting back to Maine this summer once my exams are over. Maybe I can figure this out. None of my relatives, not even my Mom, seems to know what happened. The only experience I have ever had that is anything like this was Kyle LeFrac's disappearance. That was during my junior year in high school, and I was a miserable wreck. Even now there has never been anyone else. Not really. There was a group of us in the AP courses that hung together. A big adventure was to rent an art film and crash at someone's house. The closest place of any consequence was Lewiston, if you consider Lewiston a place of consequence. I didn't. The people I hung with didn't. Maybe Boston, but New York. New York had gravitas. Anyway, except for Kyle, all I did was make out some. Honestly, that was fine with me. Sometimes I don't think I'm cut out for relationships. Oh, I worry about my Dad. We haven't heard from him.

I'm surprised how much Kyle is on my mind. I want to take you back to my time in high school when I had a thing for him. He was cute and kind of dark with black eyes. One time I asked if he was Italian. No, he said his family was French Canadian. He got the best shit. I don't know where he bought it, but it could put the two of us on some asteroid way out there, you know in a galaxy far, far away. And when we were there, we just hung. No rules, nothing, except one. I could take my pants off or he could take his off, just not at the same time. We could do that all night long. It seemed to work pretty well. I don't want to get into what I did for him, or he for me, but it was, wow, worthy of an astrolord from another universe. But I had standards. I wanted to be a virgin when I married. Of course, now I look back on this period in total disbelief. I promised my father, and Kyle said, 'No problem.' I didn't know if I would marry Kyle. He was cool to hang with, but, well, I wanted a career and maybe a house and kids. I didn't think drawing comic books or anything like that was gonna make the grade— even if it led to graphic design. It would be nice to have a place on the water like my parents' house and in the winter go to Florida or the Islands. Jesus, it gets cold here.

I wasn't sure I'd stay in Maine. My great grandfather, the first Hiram Markham, came here a hundred years ago, but these days you had to go where it was happening, regardless. I was not bad looking, and, well, I had certain skills that would please any man. I'm not talking perfect SATs—although I was close. Let's just say I was marketable, quite a nice package actually, beyond my cognitive skills. I don't mean to be snarky, but it was more than you could say for most of the girls. I was hoping to go to Harvard. I didn't know if my father, he graduated in the sixties, could help or not. But it looked good with my grades and SATs that my father was a lobsterman who went to Harvard. I was positive there weren't too many of those.

Anyway, let me give you a sample of how it went. Say, I'm texting Kyle right now:

ur pants 2 b in my pants make me pant 2 b in urs c u 2nite @8

That was a pretty typical text. Maybe his folks were in the Big Apple for the weekend, and we were going to rent a movie, go to his place, and hang. Do a little shit. Start with some kissing and go from there. Sometimes he could get a little wild. I trusted him, but I worried that he could step over the line or something, try to hurt me. So I always carried this little ice pick in my bag, not at airports or anything, but when I was with him. I snitched it from Dad's toolbox.

I should drop back some and say that I was a late child. Late, late. I am twelve years younger than Evan and Hank, probably an accident, but my parents never said so. Whatever. I'm glad to be here. Somehow I'm thinking of Latin class. Don't get me wrong. Latin was okay. It's just that Dad made me do it. Five hundred kids in my high school freshman class and you know how many took Latin? Guess. Exactly fifteen. Whoa, how dweebie was that. But there was one good thing. I met Kyle. We didn't even acknowledge each other that year, officially that is. But I did have my eye on him. He always had cool T-shirts that said things like "Babies Suck!" Well, what could you say to that? Or "Consider Badminton" and then below it "Shuttlecocks." You know, a guy had to have something on the ball to find T-shirts like that. So I was watching him. Then, the next year I got up my courage when I saw one of his shirts that said, "Virginity forever" and below it, "Fight the Big Bang Theory." I asked him where he got these wild shirts. Guess what he said. He said, "I just make things up and get someone to make me a few." That's pretty cool, don't you think? So bit-by-bit we started texting and became a number. I'm going to give you another sample, one that started out in Latin class. I am gong to call it "texting" because there was no actual sex involved.

Me: what up
Kyle: im always up for u

Me (here's where I threw in the Latin): et 2
brut
Kyle: brut aftershaving anything
Me: ur not getting anything from me (I added
more Latin) sic semper tyranis
Kyle: i want 2 b ur tyranis, rex
Me: ask me 2 hang
Kyle: hang loose i ask, rex
Me: use ur real name
Kyle: ok e rex shun
Me: way cool way 2 fast

You can see how we got to where we were.
By the way, I never sent pictures from my cell
phone, not ever. I knew that could be trouble.
They could float around for years if something
got out of hand, which I worried about even then.
There was just a lot of sizzle between us. You
ask what my father thought of all this. Well, first
you have to realize that he was forty-five when
I was born. So by the time I was in high school,
he was old. He cared. He was sweet, but he was
always preoccupied with something like the fate
of imaginary numbers in imaginary universes. He
was a live-and-let-live type and tripped out on all
he read. He read and went out on the boat with
Evan and Hank, and that was it.

Of course, that next year Kyle and I were tight.
I don't think he would have approved of texting
or what followed. And I know he would have gone
crazy with my going over to Kyle's with his parents
in New York. I would just say, I'm going out and
that was that. Honestly, I think he was relieved
when Kyle disappeared. The newspaper said he
was a "runaway." I didn't think that was so. But
it could be true. They never found him.

*　　*　　*

Which brings me back to the present. Did my Dad have Alzheimer's as the radio said? I don't know where they got that idea. He was old, but he seemed all there to me—at least when he came down to visit me at Quincy House in January. Harmless. I can't imagine his using a flyswatter. Okay, mosquitoes were something else. But he was, I guess the only word I can think of is "meek." That's all I know, except that he hasn't turned up yet. We are all so worried.

So there is one thing that is bothering me— my brothers. Could they have done something to my Dad? That's an open question. But here's what's against it. My brothers are a couple of slugs. The two of them together are soooo dumb they couldn't tell a California joke. Here's one: how many Californians does it take to have sex? Two, one to masturbate and the other to hold the video camera. Their version would be: we don't know because we've never been to California. See what I mean? They are pathetic, as if when my Mom had the twins, there were two of everything but brains. I guess together their I.Q.s are about what my Dad's is. But I want to raise the issue. If they did do it, I don't want them to get away with it. So I'm writing this into the record as a formal possibility.

The other reason I'm pretty sure they didn't do it is that I went up to Maine from Cambridge and talked to them. They were abusive and crude when I questioned them. Of course, what else would you expect? That's what you do when you don't have the firepower for arguments or discussion. You paper things over with obscenities. I kept asking them questions, and

I would get non-answers. If they were normal bright, the answers would have seemed evasive, but they would have had some. Hey, I put it up to confusion. That's the way it was growing up. They just couldn't remember things, so they would make it up. It was transparent to the rest of us. By six I was on to them. Look, none of this is clear-cut. I don't think they are bright enough to have killed our father and get rid of the evidence.

It's a judgment call. Different from the one my mother made. And the police don't have anything to go on. Until there is something specific, whether it's cell phone records or credit card receipts, or, God forbid, something worse like clothing or bones, we won't know. Maybe they are guilty of something, but there is still a possibility that nothing was done. As Uncle George said, you just can't sort this out without more data.

Well, that about wraps it up. I am finishing this in a coffee shop in Brookline—I stay out of the Cambridge scene these days, too many pretentious literary types. It's for my honors thesis. It's still a draft. I have another month. I worry that when I publish it, the University will want a piece of the IP. I also thought of writing an interactive novel where the reader gets to choose. But, well frankly, I like the control. So here's a small bone so you can feel you participated: you get to choose whether the coffee shop I am writing in right now is a chain like a Starbucks, a Peet's or a Seattle's Best or a local place like Zaftigs. And please, do not suggest Algiers, much too precious. I need some distance from Harvard Square. Or if you like, you can run a line through those choices and fill in your favorite. For example, write in Centre Street Cafe in Jamaica Plain. So that you will really feel empowered, take your yellow highlighter right now and use it any way you would like.

Professor Breathwaite has already read a draft. She called it "Tolstoy Lite." She wanted to know how I managed it. I explained that I used an iPhone app, the note function. I sat over my iPhone in coffee shops and worked the frigging screen. If I had known I was going to write a piece this long, I would have bought a Droid. A real keyboard makes a difference if you are typing something like this. All those kids were sitting with their mocha javas texting while I wrote my novel. Professor Breathwaite said, "Amazing, you really should call it, 'Tolstoy Lite.'" I rejected the title as derivative. At first I preferred "My iPhone Novel," but that didn't seem weighty enough—or honest enough. Finally, I settled on *Expiation*.

The sins of my family have ravished me, left me prostrate on a bed of shame. Only by telling our tale do I make expiation. Expiation, you say, how is telling a tale expiation? This is my confession, my public acknowledgment of our private shame. This is not public self-flagellation. No, rather I seek to put the simple truth forward as a cautionary tale—although I do not believe anyone can learn from stories like these. One cannot wage war on fate and win.

This post submission note is a summary of my thoughts now—technically it is not a post submission note because I have not yet turned in my final draft. But in this version for you, well, I want you to understand my motives. I will append a more finished version of the note to close the draft I seek to publish. But the gist of the note will be that the novel tells the harsh reality of my family, its fateful history.

Some gene, some genetic happenstance has gone haywire in every generation of my family. Can a work of art be expiation? Could a life in science expiate our acts? What if I got a Ph.D. and studied genetics or evolutionary biology to look for the cause of this obscene visitation? Or a life of contemplation in which I try to understand how the energy of sin apportions itself in this universe? Or do I simply accept the world as it is with a sigh and a nod to the series of stochastic misfortunes that has brought me to this time and place? Put another way: perhaps my brothers, Evan and Hank, are the lucky ones. A person wants to be Icarus as she seeks the sun, the Apollonian, and finds herself hurled toward the Dionysian depths.

Henrietta Markham
Cambridge, Massachusetts

XII

Barcelona

These months in Barcelona since graduation have given me time and distance for reflection and more importantly a perspective on what a year ago I thought of as expiation. How little I appreciated the role of honesty in expiation then. Icarus! Reading back over what I have written, I realize it was pure hubris to mention Icarus. My life had never taken flight. And the Apollonian—what was I thinking? I have never soared. The god of light has no use for dishonesty. It is my darkness that I needed to enter . . . but I am getting ahead of myself. What follows is a journal of how I have stumbled forward these last months—my missteps in this darkness.

They do ramble on Las Ramblas. They never scurry up and down or scamper or sashay, or strut or swagger. "Amble," that's a word that will do. Though at times we all scamper or swagger, don't we? And I no less than you. But right now I'm flat as an old tire, sitting at a table nursing a coffee, watching them amble. It's like, well,

I've dropped out beside the Silk Road with my wares and may never reach Cathay.

I am hiding and scheming. I have been trying to get my novel published. Nada, nada, nada. A complete downer. The closest I came to an agent was Heather Magnusson, who said she liked it, but she couldn't represent me, that I had a murky future. Murky! Anyway, that's fine. Who wants an agent whose name sounds like a giant hybrid flower, half Scottish and half Swedish? I sent queries on my own, and you can imagine how that went.

I've seen both versions of *The Girl with the Dragon Tattoo*. Lisbeth Salander is something else. She is one action-oriented chick. You have to admire her. Sometimes I think I am an Ivy League cross between her and Amy Winehouse, phew, who's dead. If people could read my novel, they would understand.

So after temping in New York for a few months, I needed a change and came here where it's a little humid today. Bet the frozen street performers under all that gold and silver paint are warm. They're greased enough to swim the English Channel.

Last night I had some rough sex with a visiting Israeli. Lots of cheap flights between here and Tel Aviv, he told me.

"I want to fly. Take me on a trip," I said, and he did.

"You look like Amy Winehouse."

"She's dead."

"So?"

But my point is not to ask for pity. How many novelists had to wait until their second or even third novel to get a book published, only later to have a major house bring out their first novel to great acclaim. I'm about to start a second novel here in this city fractured along linguistic lines. It's got nothing to do with Maine or Harvard or my family. I don't have a storyline yet or even all the characters. They will come as I get rolling. It doesn't have a title, but it begins: "In a large open field the Amish men sprawled disconsolate around the headless torso of a baby." *Qué triste, no?*

Not that I'm giving up on *The Lobsterman's Daughter.* I'm planning to take some Spanish classes, seduce the teacher, work my way into publishing circles here, and see if I can get someone to bring it out in Spanish or even Catalán first. It has happened before. No one is a prophet in his own land. Make that "her own land." Or is it: no one is a prophet or simply, no one is?

Just a sec. It's a text from the Israeli, "u rocked my rocks last nite can i c u before i leave"

"Sorry ones a meal"

Okay, glad that's done. Happy to see him headed for the other end of the Mediterranean. Anyway, I'll write here, first work on the Amish thing and then on whatever comes up, and of course continue to deal with the novel. Writing is like performance art on Las Ramblas. It looks like no one's moving, nothing is happening under all that body paint, yet all the while the control is ferocious.

Marco, the street artist, wants to sketch my portrait for 20 Euros. No, I told him, not without the two sun-bleached flamingos on Kyle LeFrac's lawn. They put them there for his mom's birthday and just left them. Someone must have thought they looked good. I never asked Kyle, but I know he hated them. He had taste. But well, I want the kitsch of the flamingos. In a small way they remind me of Kyle.

I'm signing off now. I want to keep this short. I don't want my non-coda wagging my non-dog of a novel.

Well, not quite. There is one more thing. Got to figure out how to make a living and begin paying back my student loans—you can be sure my genius brothers will be no help, and my mother needs what little my father had to live. So here's an idea I've been kicking around. I mean it won't make me rich like Mark Zuckerberg who left Harvard before I got there. But he and I have two things in common—each of us knows the power of the internet, and we both have a set of twins in our lives. What I've been thinking about is a string of websites that offer services I can provide and which chiefly rely on my wit and verbal dexterity. Each would be small, and I would provide product for a fee. I don't know, maybe I could attract some ads as well if the sites get popular. If I had, say, three or four and each made a little something, I would have enough to live at least and keep writing, and if I ever get my book published, I might generate enough traffic to make a decent living and, who knows, have enough business to subcontract some.

One site would provide practical help with writing for high school kids or college kids with term papers, but there is a lot of competition in that space. The real market is older people out there in the real world who want to write, say, fiction and don't want to get involved with writing workshops and such. Everybody thinks he can

THE LOBSTERMAN'S DAUGHTER~93

write a novel. It would be called "Coveryourbuts," with one "t" and the tag line would be: "Cover your buts and learn how to write clear, declarative prose that goes the distance." If I decide to do poetry too, I would have to revise this blurb, but it's a start.

A second site is a little more adventuresome. "Mindovermatter" would deal with the kinds of weird shit that most of us think about but may be too embarrassed to raise with our friends. The tag line would be: "Mind over matter: how to atomize your doubts about the supernatural and the paranormal." I think this idea has real possibilities. If I can turn around sassy, in-your-face answers that actually help people process this stuff, then there's significant potential. For example, imagine a fifth horseman of the apocalypse. That opens up lots of possibilities. In addition to conquest, war, famine, and death, what if the fifth horseman represented love? That could be a game-changer. Or in addition to parallel universes, think about the concept of perpendicular universes in which every action in every universe like perpendicular lines had the possibility of crossing into other universes. This approach, I'm sure, will have awesome appeal to the twelve to thirty set.

I'll need a few more sites before I launch, so if you have any good ideas, text me.

Some days I am so discouraged. Really, the whole website deal feels like a bunch of hollow crap. Do I really want to help dentists learn to write breathless bodice rippers? And the big thing on my mind is Kyle. His death hangs over me like a giant avenging sword. I don't have a clue how to begin. I only know that the idea of a fifth horseman whose name is love feels important—as if love, my love for Kyle LeFrac, all love is doomed because it rides with those sordid companions. Love is always in the presence of conquest and death. Shit.

XIII

April

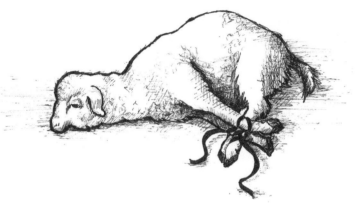

This has been a month of expiation and atonement—as close as I can come to dealing with Kyle's death. Last night I woke up with this scary dream going round and round in my head:

There was a knock at my apartment door. When I opened it, standing in front of me was the Cyclops Polyphemus with a bound lamb slung over his shoulder. He said he would like to come in and prepare rack of lamb for us. Did I mind? "No, that would be marvelous," I said. He went to the sink, drew out a long knife from beneath his cloak and slew the lamb by bleeding it from the jugular as if he were a shochet. *He asked me to open some wine—he wanted to drink as he worked—and I uncorked a bottle of Rioja I had in the pantry. We ate and drank. He was very entertaining and told me stories Odysseus had told him about the Trojan War. Then he said he was tired and needed to sleep. I explained that he could use the couch, and I went to my bedroom and latched the door. In the middle of the night he knocked and said he wanted to come in. I said, "Go back to sleep and leave in the morning." He said he was coming in, that he wanted sex. I screamed, but he easily forced the flimsy latch. I struggled and clawed him, but I was no match for a Cyclops and he pinned me down and raped me. When he was spent, he rolled off me and fell asleep. Quietly I opened the drawer of my nightstand and took out my dildo. Somehow, I was able to get to my red nail polish and paint "Kyle LeFrac" on it. When it dried, I thought, I have to protect Kyle's good name, so I slipped a condom over it. The Cyclops snored peacefully. Then I plunged the dildo deep into his eye. "This is for you, Kyle. This is for you, Simone Weil." And I ran from the room.*

I woke up shaking. At first I didn't know what to do. I tried to imagine calling my mother. That lasted about ten seconds. I realized I had no one else, no friends really, not the kind that you can call and say, "Hi. How's it going? I just called to tell you about a dream in which I painted my dead boyfriend's name on my dildo and used it to put out the eye of a Cyclops who raped me." Can you imagine getting a call like that while you are on your way to class your freshman year of law school? It would be better to coach those dentists than do that. The only person I might have been able to talk to about this was my dad, and I was certain he was dead.

I moped around for a day or two, nursing coffees on Las Ramblas and watching the tourists with their oversized straw handbags or wandering along the quay looking out at the Mediterranean and seeing nothing but a few container ships. Occasionally I stopped at one of the expensive restaurants on a wharf for *ceviche*, though I had no appetite. It was one afternoon walking back up the hill from the sea and by chance finding myself in front of Gaudi's Cathedral of the Holy Family that I was struck dumb. His magnificent vision somehow gave me permission to express my grief in my own way. If he could appropriate high funk to praise God and the Holy Family, surely I could in some small way use his approach. Which led me back to the dream.

The answer had been given to me by that dream if only I had the courage to seize it. I went into the church thinking to take two votive candles—and of course leave something in the offering box. For what I had in mind, filching seemed just plain wrong. And I worried. They didn't seem substantial enough to last twenty-four hours. No, I needed the real McCoy. I went to my iPhone and found out that there was a Chabad of Barcelona on Calle Joan Gamper. I bought two *yahrzeit* candles, which I knew would last twenty-four hours, and slipped them in my daypack. I was limp. I bagged the rest of my shopping plans and went home.

I drank a bottle of water, went to the internet and pulled up a transliterated version of *Kaddish*, the Jewish prayer for the dead, and bookmarked it. I looked around for matches, but I must have used the last of them for weed the other night. I had to light a *yahrzeit* candle for my father from a burner of the kitchen stove. With the laptop to aid my memory, I stumbled through Kaddish for him. I knew this was not mourning, not the kind I needed to come to grips with his death. It was a beginning though, a way to point myself in the direction I needed to go.

I went back to the net and pulled up "The Love Song of J. Alfred Prufrock," which I had read in a poetry class a few years ago. I needed courage, an odd thing to think that Eliot could offer, but I remembered a part of the poem that seemed important for me now. Early on he assures us that there is time for everything, including indecisions and revisions. He doesn't exactly excuse weaselly behavior like shading the truth or simply leaving out evil deeds, but certainly "revisions" would allow for second chances. That's what I felt I needed, some way to help myself confess and heal. Not an easy problem for a fallen away, unchurched Jewish woman with a lot on her plate. I went to bed drained and exhausted.

The next morning I awoke early. I was feeling stronger. I put on shorts and my running shoes and went back down to the embarcadero and jogged for forty minutes. As I looked at the piers and the water, it all felt very sterile. Odd how one anthropomorphizes—the Mediterranean seemed very noncommittal that morning—as if I had met a friendly high school English teacher who had just withdrawn his support. Then things changed. There was a light drizzle that strangely uplifted me rather than deepening my depression. I think

THE LOBSTERMAN'S DAUGHTER~99

it was that I was approaching the gloom with an endorphin high and that made a difference.

That afternoon I completed my shopping. I went to a local cheese shop, walked in and said, "*Buenas tardes.*"

A plump woman behind the counter looked me up and down. "We know only Catalán and English here. Good afternoon. What can I be of help to you with?"

"I'd like a kilo of Manchego and a big hunk of Parmesan."

"I don't understand, this 'hunk.'"

"A big piece. About like this," and I held my hands up parallel to each other.

"Some party you are having?"

"Yes, I'm having visitors, people I know in the States who will be staying with me for a day or two."

I put the cheese in my daypack and walked out.

At a nearby *panadería* I bought two large loaves of bread. I had to leave the top flap of the daypack open to accommodate them, which for the moment was fine. I didn't want to have to make a separate trip for wine, so when I got to *vinatería*, I pulled out the loaves and replaced them with three bottles of Rioja. The guy there was nice and gave me a paper bag for the bread.

Only one more thing. I went to find Vicente who hangs out on a side street off Las Ramblas.

"Listen, Vicente, I need some good shit. It's important. I have American visitors coming."

"Okay, okay, no problem. How much you want?"

"I don't know in grams. About this much," I showed him.

"How much?"

"Enriqueta, are we ever going to get together? You know . . ."

"Sure, maybe next week after they leave. How much?"

"Special price, forty Euros."

"Vicente, that's bullshit. If we are going to be friends, twenty Euros."

"No, more, maybe thirty."

I put my hand on his cheek. "Please, Vicente, twenty."

"Okay, but that's almost what it costed me."

"You are a love, Vicente," and I stuffed the pot in the pocket of my jeans. "Do you have a lighter?"

"Lighter, yes, I got. Why?"

"Can I borrow it? I'll give it back when we get together."

"OK, but when?"

"Soon. After the Americans."

When I got home, I secured the dead bolt and cut myself a piece of Manchego—it was one of the first things I learned to like here in Spain. I reasoned, what harm? I'd have plenty left for the next few days. The next part of the story, I still can't believe.

I went to the bathroom and picked up my little bottle of red nail polish. I took my dildo from the top drawer of my nightstand, and at the kitchen table I followed the instructions of my dream. I carefully letter KYLE LEFRAC along the shaft beginning at the tip and working down. I set it upright to dry as if it were a rocket on the launch pad of a NASA mission. It teetered for a second but didn't fall. I'm not all that good with my hands. *Not a very spiffy job*, I thought. The letters were crudely formed, even a little ugly—not what I intended for Kyle—but it was the best I could do. Art is one more thing for which I have no talent—and a slew of other things. I'm not very good at sports, I can't play a musical instrument, and, well, I'm in a fix if I try to fix anything. Still as I watched the red letters dry, I felt proud of the effort I had put in. The project would allow me to honor Kyle appropriately, forgive him, and hope he would forgive me. I looked at it again—Jesus, it reminded me almost of an ice pick with Kyle's name on it. I said to myself, That's okay—that's not what you meant. Trust your own decent intentions.

I opened a bottle of the Rioja and poured a generous glass. A strange thing happened. I felt the need to bless the wine the way we had learned at Hebrew school and never did at home. I held the glass toward the window and recited the blessing in Hebrew and in English. Then as if to be certain that God had heard me, I poured another glass and repeated the *Kiddush* for the wine. "Praised be Thou, O Lord our God, King of the universe who created the fruit of the vine." I suddenly had a vision of the five horses of the Apocalypse, not with individual riders, but pulling a chariot with God as the driver holding the reins. Made sense, I thought. If all things are contained in God, then he had dominion over love and hate.

Then the text alarm of my iPhone went off. "Damn."

It was the Israeli, "In barcel can i c u"

"No got americans coming"

"When"

"Never" And I put my iPhone in airplane mode.

I broke off the end of a loaf and made the blessing over the bread as if it were Shabbat. "Blessed art Thou, O Lord our God, King of the universe, who brings forth bread from the earth." Well, this was just the opposite of my quandary, which was about returning people to the earth too early. I was getting pretty hungry, so I tore off another piece of bread and cut a piece of cheese and ate them. I had no idea what had come over me. I was following my instincts about what I had to do to complete the dream in the real world. But by degrees I recognized that the three-day period I had laid out for myself was a rite of passage, an attempt to move beyond guilt.

I was grateful for my life, however imperfect it was, and I had no way to express this gratitude. I felt stumped until I remembered another blessing we had been taught and we never said at home, the *Shehecheyanu.* "Blessed art Thou, O Lord, our God, King of the universe, who has granted us life, sustained us, and brought us to this occasion." This depressed me, for God granted me life and allowed me to reach this occasion, but not the others, not Kyle.

I poured another glass of wine, rolled a joint with some of Vicente's weed, and used his lighter. Twenty minutes later I was feeling mellow, no, really mellow. And famished. I made a rough sandwich of Manchego and bread, and then another. I kept returning to Kyle. I wished he were here with me. I met a lot of smart people in college, but no one I enjoyed being with as much as Kyle. He was a cool dude. They say you outgrow high school and move on. But in this case I missed Kyle. Worse, I knew, and not deep down, but right on the frigging everyday surface that it was my fault. He would be here today, well, maybe not here in Barcelona, but alive, sustained and brought to this occasion, were it not for me. Of course, there was never any kind of funeral or memorial service. His folks kept hoping that he had run away to fulfill some grand scheme and would call or write. But he never did. Oh, Kyle, if only you hadn't broken our pact. In a way it's your fault too, but I am here mourning you, responsible or not. And you are dead, and only I know for sure.

I got up, found the other *yahrzeit* candle, put it on the stovetop, and lit it with Vicente's lighter. I called up the *Kaddish* on my laptop and struggled through it for Kyle. O, Kyle, Kyle, Kyle, wherever you are, I hope you are okay. I miss you so. You made me laugh and see things in a fresh way with your drawings and clever sayings so different from all the academic crap I learned. It's you who made me a writer. Why did it have to be without you? You are the reason for that fifth horse that God reigns over. You and people like you.

I poured myself another glass of Rioja and rolled another joint. Then I stretched out on my bed, drinking and smoking. The next thing I knew it was sometime in the middle of the night. I woke up thinking of the lamb the Cyclops had prepared for me before I blinded him and ran. I had a deep craving for Kyle, and I went out to the table and got the dildo. "Kyle, this is for you and with you," I said. I am not going to describe what happened next except to say that it was a fulsome communion. Yet I must say one more thing, which is difficult because to the wrong kind of reader it will seem titillating. When I used the dildo, it was like taking Kyle himself into me, making him part of me. Really incorporating him in the literal sense of the word. But the worst part is that it felt as if I were subsuming him—that whatever he was and whatever he stood for would be no more, not even his memory. It would all be internalized within me. His independence as a spirit would die too. Was this atonement or effacement?

When I woke up the next morning, there was bright sun coming through the window. My head felt as if someone had whacked it with a baseball bat. I brushed my teeth and looked for the Rioja. When I found it, it was empty. I opened another bottle and poured the wine into a fresh glass. I ate some bread, this time without blessing it, and some of the Parmesan. *New day, new cheese*, I thought. I went over to the *yahrzeit* candle and cupped my hands over the rising heat. "As I have blessed you, you shall bless me," I said out loud. I watched the candle flicker for a while and sat down. I started stewing over a more concrete plan for what to do when my three days of atonement were over. Nothing much came to mind except that I needed to go someplace and put some space between me and these experiences.

I turned to Kyle again. I went to the net to find stuff on Yom Kippur, the Jewish Day of Atonement, that I could use for Kyle. There was lots there, most of which I remembered from services, but none of it seemed to fit. So I sat there struggling and trying to dredge up something useful, some reading or quote or something that would commemorate Kyle and free me. Nothing felt quite right. So I sat there for a while and smoked another joint. Which only made me hungry and horny again. Which sent me back to the cheese and then back to bed.

Sometime late in the afternoon, I went out. I needed candles for my vigil. I thought about the Chabad House and rejected it. Honestly, I didn't want them to see me in my disheveled state. How could I honor Kyle if I showed up tipsy and stoned for *yahrzeit* candles? Here's where the reasoning gets a little fuzzy. Why not go back to Gaudí's Cathedral and get votive candles? I had already fulfilled the letter of the law with the *yahrzeit* candles. *Ha*, I thought to myself, *the letter with the yahrzeit candles?* I could do just as well with votive candles. I didn't necessarily need full service, twenty-four-hour-guaranteed coverage. So I went to the church and explained that I was not there as a tourist. I wanted to pray. They let me in immediately through a side entrance. I picked up two candles and left three Euros in the box. *Too much,* I thought, *but this way I honored Gaudí too.* I went to a pew, knelt and clasped my hands in front of me. I didn't know how long was appropriate. I took out my phone on the pretense of silencing it and checked out the time. Fifteen minutes somehow seemed okay. I knelt there mostly thinking of when I could leave. It seemed like forever. The only thing I was sure of was that I was glad I was not a Christian in medieval Europe. To kneel there in the winter on the cold stone floors would have been a lot.

I was glad to get back to my apartment. After the sun went down, I repeated the cycle, which didn't seem too strange for me since Rosh Hashanah—the Jewish New Year—and many other holidays, Yom Kippur excepted, are celebrated for multiple days. The only change in ritual was to use a votive candle. I figured I didn't necessarily need the intercession of a saint or the Virgin. In the modern world, isn't it all about multipurpose, multiuse materials and conventions? And I have to tell the truth here. I was meditating and seeking atonement—and the candles, the wine, the grass and the dildo all worked pretty well together.

The next morning my head was clearer. There was another text from the Israeli which I ignored. I sat quietly trying to think of a fresh path to expiation. What act or acts could I perform that would be true to Kyle and help me? Somehow, I tumbled to Simone Weil whose essay on the Iliad and force we had read in class. Oh, Kyle, it was all about force wasn't it? My not trusting you and therefore prepared. Your forcing yourself on me.

And my responding with greater force. Would it have helped to have Weil's knowledge in high school? For me, probably not. No, honestly, no. Force, evil force, was in my genes going back at least to my great, great grandfather. For my family it is some sort of persistent trait, which one cannot escape, like Tay Sachs disease or cystic fibrosis. Maybe I could have channeled it better, but I was seventeen, so young, so full of energy and myself. It's the terrible thing about sin, Kyle. Faced with the same circumstance most of us would repeat our acts. Some things are beyond learning. There is only atonement and hope. That evening I lit the second votive candle. Honestly by now, guilty or not, it was all beginning to feel a little old. But I soldiered on.

When I got up the next day, I opened the last bottle of wine and passed the third day without incident, the only difference being that I went out in the afternoon and took a long walk by the Mediterranean. The gulls kept flying in circles. I imagined they were honing in on schools of fish or the patches of refuse thrown overboard by the yachts and freighters. Hard to say. But it reminded me, not of the great cycles of our lives— the things that philosophers like Weil thought about—but of how we all chase our own tails. In our own petty ways we seek what we desire and go in circles trying to find it. I went back to the apartment, and at sundown I declared my expiation and atonement over.

Except I felt no relief. The sense of guilt and betrayal remained. And worse, the thought that the strain of violence that ran in my family permanently doomed me—that I could do something else terrible in my life.

I spent a fitful night. I got up, showered, and changed my clothes. It was early, and I walked over to a small coffee bar near Las Ramblas and stood drinking a *café con leche*. When I turned around, there was Vicente.

"*Buenos días*, Enriqueta, how are you?"

"Good, very good, actually."

"And at the present time, the Americans, your visitors, are still here?"

"No, actually only one came, an old boyfriend and he's gone."

"You are in love with him, this boyfriend?"

"I was, but that was a long time ago."

"And now?"

"And now, what?"

"What do you do, Enriqueta?"

"I have some writing I have to finish up. And then I don't know."

"Perhaps, I take you out for dinner. I can borrow a car, and we go up the coast."

"That's very sweet, but not right now." I put the lighter in his breast pocket and kissed him on the cheek. "Perhaps soon. *Hasta luego*."

"No, Enriqueta, not *Hasta luego*. *Hasta pronto*—see you soon."

Usually when I walked, I was drawn down to the sea, but that day I walked, directionless up into the neighborhoods. Somehow, I needed closure about my life and a fresh start. I was not ready for reentry. I was not sure I would ever be ready, although as I look back on that time, I realize I was being a bit melodramatic. But that's the way my life seemed—a melodrama, in which I played the innocent and the guilty, the victim and the inquisitor, the subject and the chronicler.

*   *   *

That afternoon, I set out a plan. I would spend the next month getting the chronicle you are now reading in shape and then send it back to my thesis advisor Olympia Breathwaite with a note asking her help in finding a publisher. I would post it from here but without a traceable address. Then I would go off somewhere for a while. I quickly rejected the trendy haunts. I was not going to Ibiza or Mallorca or the Riviera. I needed serious contemplation, some time away now that I had begun the process of, well, not to be coy, but I was not sure what process I had begun. I went online and found something that made me happy. There were small retreat houses all over Spain, converted cloisters or monasteries that received international visitors on a short- or intermediate-term basis. Some had focused programs, while others left you pretty much to yourself to mediate and find your own way forward.

The only point I struggled with was a title for my novel. Originally, in Cambridge, I had called the novel *Expiation*. But after I handed in my thesis, came to Barcelona, and extended it, I had settled on *Expiation and Redemption*. Yet really the process was less about redemption—who was there to redeem me anyway?—than about atonement. Did I really think that three days of reflection would allow me to rise from the death of sin to the salvation of self-knowledge? It was atonement I sought. But who would bless my offering, my atonement? I could only hope that there is some force in the universe that may accept my contrition. So at that moment I leaned toward *Expiation and Atonement*. Though as I thought more about it, that didn't seem quite right either. If I called the novel *Expiation and Atonement*, I had not really owned my actions. I had only described what I thought I had achieved. I needed a title which made my crime, my guilt, clear. I have called the novel *The Girl Who Killed Kyle LeFrac*.

I picked a retreat center in a small converted cloister in a pleasant Spanish university city. The program seemed to offer a cross between the asceticism of complete silence and the touchy-feely approach of guru-led group activities. I signed up for a three-month residency. Tomorrow I will mail this off and go to the station to catch my train.

XIV

Epilogue

A.E. had faced a crisis, a be-careful-what-you-wish-for tangle of doubt that had threatened to paralyze him. It all started when he came back from a week in Aberdeen, an assignment for his human resources job at an oil company. He had investigated a bizarre incident in which a young female engineer was assaulted on a rig and ritually murdered. It had been a trying experience, personally wrenching because of the deep sympathy he felt for her and her family, made all the more difficult by his boss's instructions to assure the company's full cooperation with local law enforcement while admitting no responsibility for the crime. Risk mitigation was what the company required of him—and as little notoriety as possible in the press. The process left him feeling unclean, as if he were coated with a film of his company's heavy crude.

One evening a few days later, still unsettled and unable to peel away the layer of filth, he headed for his favorite haunt, one of those unheralded watering holes that gives Houston much of its character. The allure of this hideaway, known as Bar Antofagasta after the hometown of its owner Florentino Burjes, rested on its potent pisco sours and a Mexican button accordion player who had appropriated most of Flacco Jiménez's and Mingo Saldívar's best material.

It was here that A.E. frequently came to brood, to unburden himself, and most of all to imagine. And so he sat alone that evening at a corner table processing the tragedy off the coast of Scotland as he worked on another pisco sour. What could be salvaged from this awful event? What lessons were there to be learned? And most importantly, what was his personal responsibility? He hated the endless stream of forms and regulations, job postings, and top-down, unimplementable initiatives that came with his HR job—one which allowed no consideration of the questions that burdened him.

The weight of his despair spilled over into his other life. Now that his agent was a hair's breadth away from placing his latest novel, perhaps there was some opportunity or some obligation here—something he might say about the poor, degraded woman who had been raped and slowly murdered. By training and temperament he was not disposed to investigative journalism. Could he tell her story by writing a novel about her,

THE LOBSTERMAN'S DAUGHTER~113

or better, one in her voice, the voice of someone whose life had been brutally and arbitrarily truncated? There was no way, he told himself, he could imagine living—and dying—in her skin. He sat alone drinking and ignoring the macabre gift fate had offered.

And now it seemed another young woman, someone A.E. did not remember seeing before, sat down across from him—simply plopped herself down at his table without asking. He sighed. What was a twenty-something year old wearing jeans and an old Harvard sweatshirt doing at his table at nine on a Tuesday evening?

"Hold on there. Just a minute," he said.

"Just a minute, what? You seem like a person I want to know better."

"Better, really?" He tried to imagine what she meant by "better" and came up short.

"You have always seemed savvy in an old-fashioned way, and I need someone to tell my story to."

"How did you find this bar? . . . And me?"

"Don't ask. It's true that Bar Antofagasta is tucked away, practically unmarked, but you are an easy mark."

"What's that supposed to mean?"

"We'll get there. Buy a girl a drink?"

"They're going to card you."

"Don't be rude."

He ordered the drink, a pisco sour.

"Okay, ah, what's your name anyway?"

"It's H.M.," she said. He paused and looked at her. "Just H.M."

"Well, H.M., where are you from and what are you doing here?"

"It's a long story, but basically I just got

back from Spain where I finished a novel that on the advice of Professor Breathwaite is called *The Lobsterman's Daughter*. I'm a writer and working on a second novel."

"So, H.M., I'm going to give you a little unsolicited advice. Give up 'H.M.' Hilda Doolittle tried something similar, and nobody reads H.D.'s poems today. Use your name, you'll see."

"It's H.M."

The waitress set down her drink.

"H.M., I have one more suggestion."

"What's that?"

"Take your drink, consider it a gift, and go sit at the bar. Maybe someone else will buy your bullshit. The only H.M. I know is my agent, Heather Magnusson."

The animation drained from her face. She squinted at him as if trying to make him out more clearly. "Magnusson, really? Look, you seem nice. It's Henrietta Markham. Okay?"

He ignored her changed demeanor. "So what's this story you feel you can only unburden to me?"

After she had finished her novel, she said she had left Barcelona and gone to a cloister on a silent retreat. She lasted only a few days. Writers didn't do well on silent retreats, she explained. They were always itching to put things down, and to write they needed the tune up of hearing other people's voices. He nodded. She couldn't tell if it was a nod of assent or a don't-feed-me-anymore-bullshit nod. Back in Barcelona, she had begun her new novel. It didn't yet have a title, but it began, "In a large open field the Amish men sprawled disconsolate around the headless torso of a baby."

He asked if she had ever been to the Pennsylvania Dutch Country. When she shook her head, he suggested that she write about what she knew. This elicited a grimace and the announcement that she had seen "Witness" at a film festival.

"Well," A.E. said, "I have heard of life imitating art and art imitating life, but it makes no sense for a writer to think that art should imitate art."

She glared at him. Her mouth ballooned with pisco sour. She considered several options for the lime-tinged liquid then swallowed it. "You've got a lot of nerve. You invited me here."

"I what?"

"You invited me here. And if you don't start treating me better, I'll leave."

"Go ahead."

She paused. "Okay, you have a point about the Amish, but it's a good story. Do you want to hear the beginning of the novel?"

"Give me a try."

Good, she would read him a bit, and she reached into an old green book bag and took out what looked like a telephone book.

"Maybe everyone gets fifteen minutes of fame, but I would like to hear the first five minutes. That will be enough."

"Enough for what?" she said.

"Enough."

Now it is true that he had had three pisco sours and that his day job was in HR for a large oil company, but it was also true that Heather Magnusson really was close to placing his latest novel. So when he stopped her after a minute and explained that she should not expect a reader to believe that a particular Amish family owned a power lawnmower—that the image stretched the reader's credulity too far—he felt he was on solid ground. She looked hurt. Could she have another pisco sour? Well, of course. He ordered two.

"You know Professor Breathwaite, my college advisor, thinks I write well. I bet she would think it's okay."

"Look, Henrietta, I don't want to hurt your feelings. Readers will accept many imaginative ploys, but not, not . . . well, it depends on the context. And here, because you already have a bunch of Amish men sprawled on the ground with a headless baby, I don't think it's a good idea to add a second iffy aspect to the story." He looked straight into her not unattractive face. "So let me think of how to say this. Normally I come here once a week or so, and I've never seen you in here. What are you doing in a strange bar with a, well, with a green book bag, wearing a Harvard sweatshirt on this particular Tuesday evening with a story about a baby's headless torso in the Amish country? If I were writing a novel, I would never try to get away with so much concentrated chance occurrence." He paused and looked at what he thought was a defiant young woman. "Tell me again why you're here."

"I told you. I just got back from Spain. The Amish thing, for the moment at least, is extraneous. Honestly, I'm here to deliver *The Lobsterman's Daughter* to you. And as for the book bag, it was my father's. He's dead. He went to Harvard and so did I. It's a keepsake. Also, I'm on my way to Mexico. To Monterrey."

"Alone? Why on earth would a young American woman want to go to Monterrey ever, and especially with the violence between the drug cartels heating up more and more each day?"

"I read a story in the newspaper about a dozen headless corpses strung up on a highway overpass. I want to see these things for myself."

"I've been there. It is not safe. Even in the best parts of the city. And certainly not for a young woman traveling alone."

"It's okay. I carry protection."

"Like what? A gun?"

"No, this," and she reached into the book bag and pulled out an old ice pick.

"For Christ's sake, you're living in some fantasy hothouse. You won't last a week. You don't even want to imagine what they will do to you. I don't know what's in this *Lobsterman's Daughter* of yours, but no matter how dark it is, it will be tame compared to what might happen down there."

"It's not my *Lobsterman's Daughter*, it's ours." He tried to interrupt, but she went on, "You know, we have been talking all night about me, and I want to hear about you."

"You're not going to clarify your statement?" he said.

"No, I told you, I want to know about you."

"It's a thoroughly boring story. I work in HR, in human resources, for a large oil company, and like you, I have a novel coming out next year. Or at least I hope I do."

"Really, that's way cool. I knew when I walked in here that sitting down at your table was the right thing to do. Tell me about the novel and what you're working on now."

"The book's called *Blowout*. It's the story of an embittered old roustabout who loses an arm in a rig accident, a blowout, and plots his revenge against the company and his fellow workers whom he thinks are responsible."

"That's a great plot. How does it end?"

"Oh, no, you'll have to read the book to find out."

"And now?" She held up her empty glass and looked at it. He motioned and flashed two fingers. "What's the new one about?" she wanted to know.

"It's a book-length poem that takes its inspiration from an actual incident that happened right here." She looked doubtful. "Really, trust me. As a writer I normally don't like to talk about work in progress, but I have a good first draft. So it feels safe. I admit that the story is odd, but one night I am sitting over there, and . . . say, there are two versions to this story. You want the real version or the literary version, you know, the writer as hero version? Never mind, the literary version's more colorful. So in walks a big biker in black leather. One thing leads to another, and we begin to talk. When I ask him his name, he says, 'Achilles.' And I say, 'Right, and mine's Patroclus.' The biker goes ballistic. His white macaw is called Patroclus, and if I know what the fuck is good for me, I'll apologize or pay a steep price. I chose the apology.

"I was pissed and swore to get even. So I sat there stewing. I was determined to have the last word, and I decided to expose this guy's raw, molten aggression, which boiled just beneath the surface. Hence the poem."

"And you think a poem is going to do it—put this guy in his place, even the score?" she said.

"I don't think martial arts is the way to go, if that's what you're driving at, not with this guy. He's one mean mother."

THE LOBSTERMAN'S DAUGHTER~119

Henrietta's nodded. "Probably not, but keep it as an option."

A.E. ignored the comment. "I'm probably a year away from finishing."

"Read me part of it? I want to hear what you do with your idea."

"I can't now. I don't have it with me. Sometimes I write in here, but not tonight."

"It's okay. I was planning to crash at your place anyway."

"A little forward, don't you think? You only met me an hour ago. And in a bar."

"No, I've had my eye on you for some time. You'll see. It will work, and you won't regret it. I promise. And one more thing: I may stay a while. I've got to admit you're probably right about the drug cartels in Mexico. It sounds pretty hairy. Yeah, the more I think about it, the more certain I am that I'll be staying a while. You could use a little lesson in humility, not to mention peaceful coexistence. At times there will be some bad shit between us, but I'm going to show you some southern comfort that's to die for. It goes way beyond the novel I'm bringing you. And you know what? I bet I can help with your Achilles story and maybe other stuff too."

Who was this bright, cheeky young woman who had sought him out at Bar Antofagasta, caught him in a vulnerable state after his experience in Scotland? He had no idea. He looked directly at her eyes. *How strange*, he thought, *it is like looking at someone wearing mirrored sunglasses*. All he could see was what seemed to be a reflection of himself.

A Guide for Readers and Book Clubs

1. Henrietta describes a photograph of her great, great grandparents Hiram and Mary Coggin Markham in great detail. How does her depiction of the photo contribute to the story?

2. Why does Henrietta treat her twin brothers Evan and Hank so harshly?

3. How does the focus of the book shift in the second half?

4. In the Epilogue Henrietta encounters A.E. What do we learn about her from this encounter and what purpose does this relationship serve?

5. Does Henrietta change over the course of the novel? Does she grow? And if so, how?